LET THERE BE DARK

TIM MCWHORTER

ISBN: 978-1-940466-84-2

Hydra Publications
Goshen, Kentucky 40026
www.hydrapublications.com

Rope Burns

"I am no witch. I am innocent. I know nothing of it."
-Bridget Bishop, June 10th, 1692, moments before being
hanged for practicing witchcraft

"The evil that men do lives after them."
-William Shakespeare, *Julius Caesar*

"A fuckin' Walgreens? Are you kidding me right now?"

Unfortunately for Sarah, no one was kidding her, least of all her fiancé, John.

"Are you sure your coordinates are right?"

The look Sarah gave him was answer enough: the slight tilt of her head, the pursing of her already thin lips and the way her eyelids drooped to the point where John wasn't sure how she was able to see through them. John knew the look well. He labored under the pretense that, in Sarah's opinion, he was the grand master of the dumb question.

Sarah turned her attention from John to the GPS on her cell. "This is exactly where the hangings were supposed to have taken place."

"And that's on good authority?"

"According to the most credible website I found." Sarah slumped further in her seat. "This is where Gallows Hill was supposed to be."

"Yeah, well," John said, looking at the brick and glass building in front of them through a rippling sheet of rain, "it's a fuckin' Walgreens now. Though it appears the marketing department chose to go with the simpler and more socially acceptable 'Walgreens' on the sign."

The rental car's wiper blades swooshed away the cascading rain, returned to their resting place and waited.

John and Sarah had been in Massachusetts for three soggy days and were anticipating their visit to Salem the most. After being there for all of two hours, things in the historic town hadn't exactly been what they had expected. Especially for Sarah. She was having to rewrite more and more of her master's thesis as the morning wore on. The topic of her essay was how the witch trials influenced the American legal system, and she had planned on utilizing information garnered from historical sites. But they were finding it difficult to locate some of these sites in person. The commercialism and capitalization on the whole witch theme, they had expected. The midnight ghost tours. The cheesy museums. The otherworldly shops on every street corner that catered to wannabe wiccans and mystics.

However, the wiping away of some of the actual history, seemingly pretending it didn't happen, was something neither of them had anticipated.

"That's progress for you." John looked out the window and tried to imagine what the area might have looked like a few hundred years ago. "Onward and upward and all that."

"Screw progress." Sarah tossed her cell onto the dashboard as the wiper blades made another sweep. Thunder rumbled in the distance. She flipped up the hood of her jacket. "I need a bottle of water anyway. Maybe something sweet to get rid of this sour taste in my mouth. You coming?"

The sound of torrential rain blew into the car's interior. Sarah was already halfway out the door before John could even turn the car off. He took a deep breath. Sarah was getting frustrated, and he could already tell that her mood, along with the weather, was threatening the vacation aspect of the trip. They only had the one day left. So far, it wasn't starting off well.

Once he had killed the engine and put his own hood up, John followed Sarah across the empty parking lot, leapfrogging the rivers that flowed through the low points of the pavement.

"Welcome to Walgreens!"

A heavy-set woman with dark-skin greeted them from behind the nearest register. She wore a red apron and her hair was pulled back. Streaks of silver coursed through otherwise black hair. She offered a smile to go with the greeting, but it was one of those smiles that people only gave because they were paid to. The nametag on her apron read "Millie." To John, Millie looked like she'd rather be anywhere else, doing anything else.

Dropping his hood, John shook the rain off his jacket and returned the smile. There had been no such acknowledgement from Sarah. She had ignored Millie's greeting while making a beeline for the snack food aisle. When on a mission, the most determined German Shepherd had nothing on Sarah. Especially when she was deep in thought. The familiar compulsion to apologize for his fiancé entered his mind, but this time, John squashed it. More pressing things were on his mind.

"Do you have a restroom?"

Millie's smile faded as if he had just asked for her credit card number. Uncertainty pulled at her brow, and her shoulders seemed to rear back just slightly. Biting her bottom lip, Millie exchanged a look with another, slightly younger, but not nearly as friendly woman who was busy restocking the do-it-yourself photo kiosk. Their eyes seemed to question each other. Each silently asked the other for guidance. After a moment, the woman at the kiosk offered a subtle shrug.

Millie returned her attention to John. Her smile returned as well, but not to the degree it had once been. "In the back. Through the storeroom and to the right." She lifted a finger, pointing toward the rear of the store. "Just be careful."

John took a step toward the rear of the store, then stopped. "I'm sorry?" The woman's last words had been spoken at a lower volume. To John, they felt more like an afterthought. Like maybe she was making the comment more to herself than him, and something about that bothered him. "Did you say, 'be careful?'"

Millie stammered. She was a child getting caught stealing cigarettes from her mother's purse. It took several seconds for her to regain her composure, fake smile and all. "I just mean, no one really uses the restroom. There are boxes and crates everywhere. You know, storage and whatnot. Just be careful where you walk."

John nodded, but still hesitated. He half expected the cashier to let out a deep breath, maybe even wipe her brow in an exaggerated manner like they do in the movies. Like she just passed a test. But ultimately, the awkward exchange wasn't John's chief concern at the moment.

He rounded a corner display stacked with Halloween candy and cut up an aisle that would lead him to the back of the store. Recognizing the orange packaging of his favorite candy, he made a mental note to pick up a bag of peanut butter cups on his way out. As much as he appreciated her offer, his idea of something sweet differed from Sarah's. Yogurt covered acai berries wasn't going to cut it for him. This day called for peanut butter and chocolate all the way.

A rumble of thunder shook the store walls. Rain pummeled the roof. The weather was turning from bad to worse, and John considered the odds of the storm passing by the time they left the store. If they were anything like the rest of their morning, the odds weren't good.

"Hey, look, hon." Sarah shouted from the next aisle over, her stint in the snack aisle atypically brief. "They're selling multi-pack condoms and lube right here on the very spot where they hung Bridget Bishop and the others. Isn't that quaint? I bet the ladies would be thrilled to know."

Not only did John not bite on Sarah's sarcastic attempt at literal gallows humor, but he hoped nobody else in the quiet store had heard her. Sarah's brand of humor was not for everyone, and the last thing John felt like doing at the moment was to have to apologize for his fiancé's inappropriateness.

"Considering what happened to them," John quipped, his arms spread wide, "I doubt the ladies would be thrilled by any of this."

Coming to the end of the aisle full of diapers, teething rings and various models of air humidifiers, John found himself at the back of the store. To his right stood wire display racks of reading glasses and canes, a long magazine stand and a twenty-something father engaged in a battle of wills with twin toddlers.

Everything to the left was decidedly less interesting.

The children frolicked like mischievous beasts, the rack of canes their toy box. John watched long enough to sympathize with the man. He appeared to have his hands full. Every time the father successfully encouraged one of the toddlers to put a cane back, the other child would pull one out. The back and forth repeated itself until John grew wary of having children of his own.

Turning left, he exited the baby needs aisle and soon saw the red door of the storage room.

John stopped short of opening the door. A feeling of being watched ran fingertips lightly along the back of his neck. He shivered. Looking up, he didn't see any video cameras present. No one else lingered anywhere nearby. No one except...

At the other end of the aisle, the toddlers had ceased their engagement—one in mid retrieval of a cane, the other skipping just out of reach of the father. Both stared blankly at John. No expressions populated their cherubic faces. No words passed between them. Even their gleeful smiles were gone. The two watched John as if they knew his future and simply wanted to bear witness.

It all gave John the creeps. He turned away and pushed open the red door.

Millie hadn't lied. There were cardboard boxes sitting here, there and just about anywhere someone could find a place to set one. A maze of printer paper cartons stood between him and anywhere he wanted to go, their lids secured with clear packaging tape. Two stacks of blue Pepsi 2-litre crates created twin towers as tall as John. It all left just enough room to walk on his search for the restroom. He almost missed the nondescript white door. A stockpile of mismatched boxes hid it well. If John hadn't known any better, he'd have sworn someone had purposefully blocked the door to the restroom so that no one could use it.

The door squeaked when he opened it, adding more fuel to the feeling that, in fact, nobody did use the restroom.

Stepping through the doorway to the windowless room felt similar to how John imagined it must feel stepping into a prison cell. Lonely. Cold. The room had the feeling of being both over and underused at the same time. One of the two overhead lights was burnt out, giving the already drab and colorless room a noticeably depressed and dismal look. The paper towel dispenser hung crooked. The bottom of the soap dispenser was crusted over with blue goo. It was the same blue goo that had dripped down onto the countertop and crystalized. Everywhere John looked, a layer of dust coated the forgotten surfaces.

"Damn." John closed and locked the door behind him. "Doesn't anyone around here ever need to take a leak?"

The restroom's condition tweaked John's germophobic compulsion, but his need to answer nature's call remained a higher priority. At least there was toilet paper available. And plenty of it.

Stepping up to the toilet, John unbuttoned his jeans. His zipper was halfway down when he thought he heard a whisper. His fingers froze in mid zip. His ears alert. John stood motionless and listened for the whisper to come again. The sound had been undeniable. So he thought. Was it possible he was hearing things? Had to be, right? Knowing full well he was alone in the tiny room, John decided there was no other explanation. He allowed himself to breathe. He continued unzipping his jeans.

"In-no-cent."

The whisper came louder the second time, drawing out the word so that the last syllable didn't end, but merely faded into nothingness. The voice was genteel, female and most certainly meant for John's ears.

"Sarah?" John's voice echoed in the tiny room. He turned his attention to the door. "Are you messing with me?"

John leaned down and peered through the slit under the door. The space was thin and narrow, offering only the tiniest of glimpses into the outer room. With no break in the light, it didn't appear that Sarah, or anyone else for that matter, stood on the other side. After a moment of prolonged silence, John had no alternative but to dismiss the sound as nothing more than being in an unfamiliar place. After all, this location was already shrouded in mystery. A healthy dose of paranoia was to be expected.

With his jeans around his ankles and his cell phone in hand, John went about his business.

"salem so-so thus far," the tweet started. "went to site of executions only to find jimmy caps and peanut butter cups #isnothingsacred"

He had just hit the send button when the lone light in the restroom flickered. John looked up at the bulb, half expecting it to go out. It would play along with the rest of the luck he was having this morning. Or lack thereof.

John held his breath, and after several seconds, was pleased when the light remained on.

"Thank you, God." John set his cell phone atop the toilet paper dispenser and relaxed.

Then, as if the universe had the ability to detect sarcasm, the light bulb went out.

"Son of a bitch."

In the world outside the Walgreens, thunder clapped and rain battered the roof.

In John's world, there was nothing but darkness.

"Would it have killed them to put in a window?"

John felt around in the pitch black. His hand searched the wall for the toilet paper dispenser and the cell phone that rested on top. His fingertips had no sooner grazed the top of the metal box when a crash broke the silence. John counted three subsequent bounces as his cell phone skittered across the floor. The tinkling of glass shattered his spirits.

"Shit."

Overhead, the light bulb flickered back to life.

As he searched the floor for his cell, John expressed thanks to anyone who might be listening for the ability to see. Unfortunately, his relief was short lived. The bulb immediately began to blink again. The filament twitched as it struggled to stay lit.

"Screw this." John reached for his jeans. "I've held it this long."

Movement out of the corner of his eye stopped his progress. Beside him, the large roll of toilet paper turned on its spindle. The motion was subtle, but without question. Where the end of the roll was once hidden, two full squares of tissue now hung free and ready for use.

John dropped his jeans and sat up straight, shying away from the dispenser.

"What the—"

Before any more words could escape his lips, the roll of toilet paper once again took it upon itself to turn. This time, it didn't stop. Toilet paper flew through the air in a graceful ribbon before giving in to gravity and plummeting to the floor. Thin white single-ply accumulated at John's feet. With each passing second, the mound grew while the size of the roll shrank. Stunned and confused, John sat without motive, mesmerized.

The rain continued its assault.

The light bulb flickered.

Toilet paper spewed from the dispenser's mouth at an alarming rate. It was as if someone had hooked a motor to it. With the last of the tissue floating gracefully to the floor, the cardboard spool continued to spin for a few more seconds before coming to rest. What began as a full roll had emptied itself in a matter of seconds.

John tried to make sense of what had just happened as the room fell into a state of hushed calm. The still, a stark contrast to the earlier mayhem. The lightbulb stopped flickering, but not in the way John would have liked. Darkness filled the room.

Anxiety fueled the voice in John's head, urging him to get the hell out. Something was seriously wrong with the place. The light bulb. The toilet paper. None of it made sense. He should leave, the voice instructed, before anything else happened. He wanted to comply. He wanted to move, but his body wouldn't respond. He sat frozen, a growing fear stopping him. He was a wax statue.

When the calm stretched out for several moments, John allowed himself to relax. Did he even believe in the supernatural? He took a breath. He commenced searching for his cell with his foot.

"In-no-cent."

John bolted upright.

The word began echoing all around him, soon coming from more than one voice. What started as whispers grew in volume. Shouts soon filled the room. Angry bellows from the mouths of women, both young and old, their voices like the painful cries of an injured animal.

"In-no-cent!"

John put his hands over his ears, attempting to ward off the assault. It wasn't enough. Not even close. He could feel the bellows in the back of his skull as much as hear them. They resonated through his body like a shiver, striking every nerve.

When removing himself from the situation became more imperative than blocking out the voices, John lowered his hands and reached for his jeans. His eardrums immediately suffered the consequence. The sound like a freight train in his head. His heart thumped in his chest. He pulled up his jeans.

Once zipped and buttoned, John turned in the direction of the door, using outstretched hands to navigate through the dark.

A crunch under foot. His cell. He reached down and retrieved the ruined device. Bits of broken glass and plastic fell by the wayside. The screen remained dark. John slipped the phone into his pocket.

The light bulb flickered back to life.

The voices fell silent. Only the drumming of rain remained, the pitter patter a bit softer, the rhythm more resolute. However, it did nothing to ease John's nerves. The damage was already done. He approached the sink.

"Dude, splash some water on your face." He turned his head side to side. In the mirror above the sink, his reflection followed suit. His face looked pale and gaunt, his eyes weary. "You'll be alright. You're a little messed up right now, but you'll be alright."

After turning on the faucet, John cupped his hand under the flow of water. He was already doubting his own assurances when he suddenly found it difficult to take a simple breath. Air wasn't flowing as naturally as it should. A tightening sensation started forming around his larynx. He gulped air that wouldn't go down. The pressure against his throat soon encircled his entire neck.

The dusty mirror itself shed no light on the situation,

offered no explanation. There was nothing wrapped around his throat that John could see. He searched frantically with hands that came up empty.

John's feet left the floor. Gravity gave way to something altogether unnatural as he began rising into the air. *Lifted* into the air. By his neck. The pressure around it tightened. Panic set in, and he began to kick the open space below. His shin connected sharply with the edge of the countertop. Pain shot through his leg. He tried to scream. His attempt failed.

By the time John stopped rising, he hovered a good three feet above the ground. The top of his head nearly touched the ceiling. Below him only empty space where he continued to flail his legs. Over and over again, his feet connected with the edge of the countertop. Pain no longer registered. It wouldn't have mattered if it did. The harsh strikes against the laminate were the only sound he could produce. He hoped it was enough. His senses were dulling, his vision becoming cloudy.

Breathing became a memory.

The next voices John heard were calling his name. Somewhere outside the fog that filled his head. Shouts of "John" reached his ears. They weren't the same voices that had so passionately expressed their innocence moments earlier, though their urgency was similar. Hands pummeled the restroom door.

Still, all activity outside of John's own fight for survival was relegated to the back of his mind.

Panic maintained a grip he couldn't wriggle free of. Terror threatened to squeeze the life out of him before the lack of oxygen could. The urge to swallow became a desperate one. Attempting to only made matters worse. Air wouldn't come. Air wouldn't go. The only result was increased crushing pain. No matter how hard he tried, how much he struggled, John found himself unable to stop the black cloud from enveloping him. His final thought was of Sarah and how disappointing the trip had been.

John's legs were weak and gave immediately, so it was his tailbone that took the brunt of the fall. The unseen force that had pulled him into the air—*what the hell was it*—abruptly released its grip. The pressure around his throat vanished, leaving only residual pain. He gasped and sucked in air. Sweet oxygen flooded his searing lungs. And as John sat on the dirty floor, clarity returned and his mind cleared.

The door to the restroom flew open.

Sarah stood in the doorway. The woman whose nametag read "Millie" stood looking over her shoulder. A set of keys hung from Millie's hand.

"John!" Concern filled both Sarah's voice and face. "What the hell? Are you okay?"

John scrambled to his feet, ignoring the torment coursing through his lower back. He shot a glance up at the ceiling. Not surprisingly, he saw nothing. It was just a ceiling, white and featureless, save for a few yellow water stains. The mound of toilet paper, too, was gone. A fresh roll of crisp, white tissue hung in the dispenser just waiting to be used.

As if it always had been.

"Get me out of here," John said, though it came out as more of a raspy murmur than an intelligible string of words.

Sarah stepped back from the doorway, allowing John through. After exchanging a confused look with Millie, Sarah followed her fiancé. One behind the other, Sarah and John made their way down the aisle toward the front of the store.

In his haste, John didn't pick up that bag of peanut butter cups. He didn't even bother covering his head as he stumbled out into the rain. By the time John reached the rental car and unlocked the doors, he was soaked through. Rain found its way inside his collar, running in streams down his back.

Yet it didn't bother him. None of it did. It felt good to be out in the elements. So much so that he took a moment, eyes closed, and turned his face to the sky. The steady rainfall pelted his skin. As much as possible, he allowed it to wash away the residue from the last few minutes.

"John?" The sound of his fiancé's voice brought him back around. "John, are you okay?"

He looked across the roof of the car. Rainwater ran off the front of Sarah's hood like the gutter on a porch. Despite the rain falling between them, John could see the lines of concern that still creased her face.

He took a moment to slick his wet hair back and wipe his forehead. "I'm fine. Just goin' a little crazy is all."

Sarah's façade of worry began to crack. She offered a subtle smile. "Well, this town is certainly no stranger to crazy." On that note, Sarah opened the car door and disappeared inside.

John couldn't help but chuckle. He wasn't sure he would ever be able to explain to Sarah what happened in the Walgreens restroom. Hell, he was struggling to comprehend it himself. Maybe his attempt at a joke held more truth than he realized. Maybe he *was* going a little crazy.

Once the car doors were closed and the weather was shut out, John pulled his jacket up and over his head. He shook the rain off and tossed the jacket into the back seat.

"What's that?" Sarah reached over and began fumbling with the collar of John's damp shirt.

"What's what?"

"It…it looks like…" Sarah cautiously touched her fingertips to John's neck. "a rope burn."

John flinched. His skin was tender where Sarah touched. He adjusted the rearview mirror to get a look for himself.

"Son of a bitch." A red and purple abrasion formed a perfect circle around his neck. John touched it again to verify that it still hurt. It did. He sat back in his seat and looked at Sarah. "I think I've got a new angle for your Masters thesis."

————

"Rope Burns" is the result of a road trip I took through New England in October of 2014. Although Salem, MA, was indeed one of the highlights of the trip, (after all, I am a fan of history who happens to write horror) it was not without its disappointments. Like Sarah in the story, I fully expected the nauseating amount of commercialism that had sprung from the town's history, namely the witch trials. What I was not expecting was the lack of preservation of some of the buildings and sites where said history had taken place. Admittedly, many of the descendants of those involved in the witch trials would probably just soon forget it ever happened. The Salem Witch Trials of 1692 did not make for a gold sticker stop on our nation's timeline. Still, it was disappointing not to see more of that history preserved. Regardless how morbid and shameful some may perceive it to be.

No one really knows the true location of Gallows Hill, the area where the hangings took place. Many so-called experts have their opinions, but there is no consensus among them. If you scour the internet, you can read all of the theories and potentially narrow the location down to a handful of possibilities. One would think that the location where those innocents were senselessly executed would not be so clouded in mystery. One would think it would be a relatively well-known place. But it is not, for better or for worse.

I had a conversation with a very nice, and seemingly knowledgeable woman we met while exploring The Burying Point Cemetery. As any good tour guide should be, she was dressed in 17th century garb and knew many of the stories of those buried in the cemetery who'd had a hand in the trials. When the conversation turned to the hangings, I asked about the execution location. She told us that the spot she has always heard about is a few miles out of town, and that a Walgreens had been built over the site. Now, whether or not that is indeed the spot is anyone's guess.

But I would say that if there was ever a place that might be teaming with malevolent spirits, it seems the site where innocent people were falsely accused of witchcraft and executed would be a logical place. Specifically, the very spot that gave Gallows Hill its not-so-illustrious name.

Even if it is a fuckin' Walgreens now.

The Company You Keep

"Smoke?"

Tony held the cigarettes out to Visili, who sat like a statue in the passenger seat. He had spent much of the drive so far staring out the window at the passing night. There wasn't much to look at—a nonstop caravan of shadowy trees and vacant fields—but if it kept the scary guy in the grey suit content, then that was just fine with Tony.

Visili moved nothing but his lips when he answered. "No."

Tony shrugged. He used his thumb to flip open the silver cigarette case he'd won off of Riggs in a poker game. It was a nice case, vintage scrolled design with Riggs' initials engraved on the front. When Riggs' disappeared, Tony thought about having the case refinished and his own initials engraved on it. Maybe someday. He popped a slender hand-rolled job into his mouth and immediately savored the taste of Burley on his tongue.

"No." Visili repeated. This time Vincent Dominico's

Chief "Getting Shit Done" Officer turned to face Tony. "I mean no cigarette for you, too. Put it away."

Tony took his eyes off the road. He met Visili's gaze for two seconds before the guy turned his attention back to the window. And two seconds was enough. Visili's steel grey eyes exuded their usual cold gleam, issuing a warning that didn't need verbalized. Tony would have to tread lightly.

"Seriously? Why?"

Visili shrugged. "Not your car." It was a simple argument. Effective.

Shaking his head, Tony spat the cigarette back into the case and tossed it onto the center console.

Tony was starting to sweat. The air inside the car was warm and grew more stifling by the minute. He lowered his window about halfway. The cool night air wasted no time rushing in.

Disappointed as he was, Tony couldn't argue with the man's logic. This wasn't Tony's car. His car was in the shop. In the meantime, Mr. Dominico had stuck him with this inconspicuous blue Chevy. The fact that it had been lifted from some poor nine-to-five bastard with a fast food addiction was painfully obvious by the stack of napkins in the glovebox and the ever-present stench of grease and stale fries. Which was why Tony couldn't see the harm. A little cigarette smoke wasn't going to cause any more damage that daily trips through a drive thru hadn't already done. Dominico's automotive guy said it would take a couple days to replace the windows in Tony's Mercedes. It felt like weeks. Ten minutes behind the wheel, and Tony already hated this car. Compared to his Mercedes, the Chevy took curves like a fat kid on a tricycle.

Tony could've used that smoke, too. He was nervous as all hell riding along on a job with the infamous Visili Prek. The Albanian. Who wouldn't be? Especially after the way

Tony had fucked up and gotten the boss's girlfriend jacked. Sitting in Mr. Dominico's office, photographs of a bound and gagged Ava spread out on the old man's desk, Tony was lucky his boss didn't order Visili to kill him right there on the spot. But Tony also knew the possibility was still there. Always would be. The company you keep and all that.

"You catch the Tigers game last night?" he asked, turning the radio on. The voice coming through the speakers was ranting about Detroit's latest trade. According to the announcer, it promised to sink their season.

Visili's answer was to reach up and turn the radio off.

"Not a big baseball fan, huh?"

"Just drive."

Tony shook his head. Scary guy or not, Visili's shit was getting old.

"Or maybe you just don't like me." Tony offered a chuckle, a veiled attempt at camouflaging his unease. He sat straighter in the seat.

This time the man smiled when he looked over at Tony. "Don't forget, Mr. Malone. I suggested killing you. For Ava. Better you just drive."

With a hard swallow, Tony did as he was told, his hands at ten and two, his wide eyes forward. As the Chevy's headlights stretched out over Route 38, Tony took a trip back in time. As painful as it was, he thought back to earlier in the day and how he'd gotten himself in this situation in the first place...

Her body was amazing. Tits, ass, the whole works. Tony could see why his boss kept such close tabs on her. Any guy in Detroit would be happy to walk into a club with a

Russian beauty like Ava on his arm, and most wouldn't let a little thing like being a mob boss's girlfriend get in their way. She was *that* alluring. Her milky white skin was guaranteed to cool you down on a hot summer day. Silky blonde hair pulled into a ponytail trailed down to the small of her back. The tattoo on her left shoulder of a brown bear wearing a Russian military *ushanka* would have been easily forgettable on a guy, but looked completely badass and even a little sexy on her. Not to mention the fact that she was rumored to come from a very well-connected family of Russian assassins.

The general consensus was that Ava Stepanov wasn't the type of woman who needed protecting.

But that was Tony's job, nonetheless, and not an easy one at that. His orders were simple enough: pick up Ava from her downtown salon and ferry her to his boss's house out in Grosse Pointe. A seemingly painless job made less so by Ava herself. She liked to flirt with the younger guys in Vincent Dominico's crew, test their loyalty. Case in point: she should have been sitting in the back seat of Tony's silver Mercedes sedan, not up front with him. But since he didn't have eyes in the back of his head, what fun would that have been for the seductive Ava? Tony played it cool, though. He knew what happened to the last guy who thought he could sample the forbidden fruit.

Well, that wasn't exactly true. Nobody really knew what happened to Riggs. They just knew he wasn't around to play seven-card stud on Friday nights anymore.

But here was Tony, pulling up to a red light only a couple miles from his boss's house, and the woman he was tasked to protect was literally undressing in the passenger seat. She started with the top, pulling it up over her head, revealing nothing more than what God had blessed her with underneath. He wasn't surprised, and even though he knew it could be dangerous, Tony gazed upon perfection from the corner of his eye.

Ava turned around in the seat, stuck her ass in the air, and started rustling around in one of the bags she'd had when Tony picked her up. Bags of all sizes filled the back seat of his Mercedes. Fancy white, silver, and pink paper bags full of clothes that Tony's girl could probably never afford. He could see Ava's ass wiggling back and forth in the rearview mirror. She looked like an excited puppy nosing through the trash.

After taking longer than needed, Ava returned to her seat.

Raising an expensive-looking white top to her mouth, she used her even whiter teeth to rip the price tag free. Arms in the air, Ava started slinking into the top, thrusting her breasts forward as she did. Really playing it up. Tony couldn't help but snicker at the ridiculousness of the whole act.

But ridiculous or not, it didn't stop his mouth from drying out or his hands from growing clammy. Tony finally turned away. *What's taking this light so fucking long?* The sooner he delivered this package, the better. He had only been Mr. Dominico's wheelman for a few months and already had his sights set on bigger things within the team. And no flirty Russian chick was going to screw it up for him.

Nice tits or not.

The driver side window exploded. Slivers of glass stung the left side of Tony's face. A second later, a black leather fist gripping a blackjack shot through the opening and unhinged his jaw. The force threw Tony against the center console between the seats. The bolt of pain was immediate. His ear began to ring.

Ava screamed as glass shattered on the passenger side. A

similar black leather glove reached through the ruined window and started fumbling with the lock on the passenger door. An instant later, the door flew open and two black gloves grabbed Ava by the arms. She was wrenched from the car with her new white top still covering her head like a hood. The last thing Tony saw of Ava were her perfectly dainty feet with purple toenails wrapped in a pair of white sandals.

Tony's eyes drifted closed as he fought to stay conscious. His foot slipped off the brake and the Mercedes idled into the intersection. As a chorus of car horns started chirping, Tony spent his remaining moments trying to figure out what he had done wrong. But it didn't matter.

Ava was gone.

And in that instant, with full clarity, Tony Malone knew he was a dead man.

The Chevy rambled along Route 38 whose pavement needed resurfacing, but whose lack of traffic made it a low priority.

Tony rubbed his still swollen jaw with one hand while drumming his thumb on the steering wheel with the other. The meeting in Dominico's office that afternoon had been tense, to say the least. *Someone's gonna die for this,* Dominico had said. *Someone's gonna die badly.* Then, Tony's boss had sent him on this errand with Visili to teach him how to demand respect from their enemies. *It will be a good lesson, Mr. Malone. One you will, and must, learn if you are ever to chauffer me or anyone dear to me ever again.* Tony heard the words as they were spoken, but interpreted them as they were truly intended: if you want to spend another day above ground.

They motored along, mile after nighttime mile in silence. Signs briefly flashed through the headlights before flying past. Tony didn't bother reading them. He didn't know what he was looking for anyway. His instructions were simple and to the point. *Just drive,* Visili had said. So that's what Tony did.

He drove.

In the passenger seat, the man of few words continued to ride in silence. The dim blue light from the dashboard gave his face an even harder edge. His cool grey suit was tight in all the most intimidating places. A thick patch of bushy black hair stuck out of the top of his button up. It provided the perfect backdrop for the gold cross that hung around his neck.

As they passed a stiff-legged deer gracing the shoulder of the road, Tony wondered just how religious the hired enforcer could be. He also wondered if Visili was packing at the moment. Tony concluded that he probably was. After all, wasn't it the tool of his trade?

They were a good twenty miles outside of the city before Visili spoke again. "Slow down. Turn right up here."

Tony slowed the Chevy. He turned onto a lane that used to be gravel, but now only resembled a gravel drive in the few spots where there still was some. Dirt, overgrown grass, and long-lost leaves had taken over. Wider than your average driveway, there was enough space for two cars to pass by one another. The path entered into a dense clump of trees.

And Tony's mouth turned to desert sand.

The trees themselves weren't a good sign. They separated their destination from the main road and anyone who might be passing by. Generally, in this type of situation, seclusion wasn't a good thing. He'd heard the stories. He'd seen the movies. Tony's heart rate increased by a tick.

What the hell could they be retrieving from a house all the way out here?

Gravel crunched beneath its tires as the Chevy crept through the trees.

A moment later, at least one of the mysteries was solved. The lane was wider than most driveways because it wasn't a driveway after all. It didn't lead to a house. The makeshift lane emptied onto a large gravel parking lot the size of a football field. Row after row of four-foot-tall metal poles stuck up from the ground, each leaning this way or that. Dull grey boxes hung in pairs at the tops. In some instances, only one remained while some posts were naked altogether. On opposing ends of the parking lot, two tall white movie screens stood facing each other in a standoff, frozen in time. A small building sat in between. The roof buckled in the center and hardly looked weatherproof. Windowless and missing most of its doors, the concrete block structure appeared vulnerable and unlikely to defend itself should the need arise.

"Oh, shit," Tony chuckled, flipping on the car's high beams. "An abandoned drive-in movie theater." *Oh, shit,* Tony thought. *An abandoned drive-in movie theater.*

In the woods.

In the middle of nowhere.

Tony steered the car through the rows of metal poles and toward the deserted building. Swinging the car around, he pulled up beside the concession stand. He put the car in park. For security purposes, Tony left the engine running and the headlights on, pointing back toward the entrance.

"Turn off the car."

Tony's first instinct was to argue for leaving the car running. He didn't follow it. Instead, he wiped his clammy hands on his pants before following Visili's latest order.

Once the engine was cut, everything fell silent, both inside and outside the car. Tony thought he could hear the faint sound of crickets, a sound seldom heard over the frenzied cacophony of the city. But he couldn't be sure. It could have very well been a case of twenty-year old nostalgia from a time when going to the drive-in with his parents was the highlight of a ten-year old's week.

Somewhere in the night, an owl sounded its familiar call.

Visili checked his watch, then their surroundings. "Be right back," he said, unbuckling his seatbelt. "Gotta take a piss." The Albanian exited the car and made his way around to the back side of the building.

Tony let out a long and exhaustive breath. His hands trembled. His heart raced.

A natural born tension had permeated the car since picking up Mr. Visili Prek, and Tony was thankful for the respite. He took the opportunity to sort through his thoughts. All manner of voices in his head offered their two cents on the situation, dolling out unsolicited advice. The loudest among them told him to run, that they weren't really there to retrieve anything. The voice probably wasn't wrong. It was the oldest trick in a very well-worn and bloody book: convince the dead man walking that he wasn't about to die right up to the point that he did. Tony's best bet was to just drive off and leave his presumed killer behind. It didn't matter where he went, just disappear. But Tony also knew that he could never stop running if he started. No corner of the Earth would be safe. No matter where he went, the odds of Vincent Dominico finding him lied somewhere between pretty damn good and absolute certainty. And then Tony really would disappear.

Just like Riggs.

Tony swiped his cigarette case from the console and

climbed out of the car. He was long overdue for a smoke, and the more his mind worked, the more his body craved it. Leaning against the hood of the Chevy, he placed a cigarette between his lips. His cheap, gas station lighter was shameful in comparison to the silver case, but it did the job. Tony lit the cigarette and drew in a deep lungful. Eyes closed and head back, he let sweet nicotine do its thing. He repeated the process of turning tobacco to ash, wishing the whole time that the moon would come out and shed some light on the situation.

But Tony didn't have time to ruminate the merits of lunar illumination. He had just flicked a world record length of ash onto the ground when he heard the low moan of a car engine. A moment later, a pair of headlights shown through the trees as a vehicle crept its way up the lane.

Tony released a lungful of smoke into the night air.

For all the good the cigarette had done, it was pissed away just as quickly. Tony watched a long black sport utility vehicle emerge from the trees and roll onto the lot. It was a full-size SUV. Intimidation on four wheels. The kind government officials rode in while parading through the murderous streets of some third world country. The large body was freshly washed and waxed, its windows blackened. The grill like a gaping shark's mouth. The beast of a vehicle swam its way past the rows of speaker posts.

"Shit." Tony looked to the concession stand. "Hey, Prek! Give it a shake and hurry your ass up." Tony let out a long and exhaustive breath. As disquieting as the SUV's entrance was, he was all about silver linings. At least Visili hadn't brought him all the way out here just to put a bullet in his back. There was a mission in place after all.

The heavy front end of the SUV swung around until it faced the Chevy head on. It came to a stop, leaving just enough space between them to permit a quick escape should the need arise. It was a practice Tony was well acquainted with. Wheelman 101. The SUV cut its headlights but not its engine. Yet another time-honored maneuver.

Only the Chevy's headlights lit the bed of gravel between the vehicles.

"Prek!" Tony's eyes didn't stray from the SUV. "We got company!" His heart was about to burst through his chest. Nothing else, it was taking years off his life. He was used to simply being the wheel man in these situations. His job was to sit back and wait for the shit to go down so that he could get everyone out safe in as short a time as possible. He wasn't comfortable being front and center of the shit going down. Especially when he didn't have a rat's ass idea what this meeting was even about. Prek was supposed to be retrieving something. Tony was clueless as to what that something was. Any information beyond that was apparently above his pay grade.

Tony dropped what remained of his cigarette onto the ground and snuffed it with the toe of his Florsheim.

The front passenger door of the SUV opened slowly, followed a moment later by the driver side door. Highly-polished shoes emerged from both sides. The men they belonged to remained shielded by the large doors.

And Tony wished he had time for another cigarette.

The two men eventually meandered around the SUV's doors and toward the front of the vehicle. Each wore what looked to be dark grey suits. Each looked expensive. All other details eluded Tony due to the poor lighting. The Chevy's headlights didn't quite reach that far, and the moon seemed content to remain hidden behind a cluster of clouds.

Speaking of hiding…

Where the hell was that Albanian asshole?

Tony wanted to shout to Visili again, but refrained. It didn't seem wise now that the two men were within earshot. How would that look? He didn't even know whether these guys were friend or foe. For all he knew, shouting out like that might spook them into action. And action, given the circumstances, would more than likely be a bad thing. Visili may be packing, but Tony wasn't. He took a deep breath and let it out slowly.

Tony stepped to the front of the Chevy.

"Gentlemen." Tony's voice was firm and echoed in the emptiness. The composure it displayed was a lie, but hid the truth well. It appeared as if the man standing on the driver's side gave Tony a nod, but he couldn't be sure. It was difficult to keep eyes on both men at once.

"Got the money?" the passenger said. The man's voice was plain, indistinguishable.

But it wasn't the man's voice that started Tony's stomach churning. It was what he had said. *Money?* Visili was to retrieve something, but there'd been no mention of an exchange taking place that Tony had heard. Nor did Visili bring along a duffle or briefcase that Tony had seen. Yet, these two men were expecting money from them. More specific to the situation, they were expecting money from *Tony*.

His hesitation must not have sat well with the two men.

Slowly and in unison, as if they'd practiced this specific scenario, the two men unbuttoned their jackets. Each pulled the left side back, revealing not only pressed white shirts, but shoulder holsters. Tony couldn't see what kind of guns they held, but some caliber of firepower was implied.

And here Tony stood without even a holster to brandish, much less a gun.

Son of a bitch.

"Hey, listen fellas." Tony put his hands forward. "I was told—"

A mournful and high-pitched howl split the night like a cleaver. Long and drawn out, it came from behind Tony. A tickle ran up his neck. A shudder flowed down his back. When he turned and looked up, his jaw dropped. A cold sweat engulfed his body.

Its dense, black and grey fur shrouded a muscular form silhouetted against an emerging moon. Its snout, long and squared, was raised to the sky. But that's where the traits of a normal wolf ended. This wolf stood atop the roof of the concession stand. This wolf *stood* on its back legs. Like a man. As it spread its arms and expanded its broad chest, a second bestial and bone-chilling howl filled the night.

The wolf leapt from atop the building without warning, landing on the roof of the Chevy.

Tony's eyes doubled in size. He took a step back.

The wolf hovered over him, mere feet away. Tony gasped at the sight. The threat of being devoured by the wolf's yellowed teeth sent him stumbling to the ground. From his backside, Tony stared up at the primal being, mouth agape.

But the wolf didn't stay on the Chevy long enough to acknowledge Tony, much less devour him. It leapt over him. Its feet had hardly hit the ground when the wolf darted toward the unsuspecting SUV with the zeal of a predator in pursuit.

Both men went for their guns. The passenger pulled his from its holster just as the wolf descended upon him. A scream of utter terror tore through the night. The wolf took the man to the ground. More screams of pain and rabid growls followed. The man kicked his feet and thrashed his arms, but it wasn't enough.

A gunshot rang out as the driver fired wildly in the wolf's direction. His aim was rushed. The bullet ricocheted off of the SUV's hood, stripping it of paint. A second shot took out a headlight. The wolf was on the ground, well out of the man's view. Even attempting a shot was pointless.

When the screaming finally stopped, only guttural utterances made their way to Tony's ears.

He scrambled to his feet. His eyes remained glued to the devastation taking place beside the SUV. Tony wanted to run, to drive, to do something. Wanted to shout out to Visili. The only thing he didn't want to do was draw attention to himself. So far, it was as if the wolf hadn't even noticed him. *But, how?* Whatever the reason, Tony preferred to keep it that way.

The wolf whipped its head from side to side, splaying flesh and blood onto the ground and along the side of the SUV. The man was long dead, and once the wolf was finished with him, it sprang onto the SUV's hood. Even from his vantage point, Tony could see red glistening on the wolf's muzzle.

The driver shouted with terror as he climbed behind the wheel. He reached for the door, but the wolf was too quick. The driver lost his arm just below the elbow. Shrieks erupted from inside the SUV. The wolf spat the arm onto the ground and followed the shrieks to their source. Horrific sounds the likes of which Tony had never heard came from inside the SUV. Screams. Snarls. Wails. Growls. The vehicle rocked from side to side. Red blood painted the windshield.

The door behind the driver flew open. A third man, this one in a black suit, emerged from the SUV. Without hesitation or pretense of aiding his partners, the man took off on foot, making a beeline in Tony's direction.

The wolf lunged from the SUV, appearing from behind the driver side door.

"No!" Tony shouted. The man was going to bring the wolf right to him.

After a short series of feral barks, the wolf gave chase.

Run, dammit! But Tony was too in awe to heed his own advice.

The man in the black suit, however, ran like his life depended on it. Pointing his gun behind him, he squeezed the trigger repeatedly as he weaved his way through the obstacle course of metal posts. Miraculously, several of the shots hit their mark. The wolf's shoulder and abdomen jerked from the impacts. But the damage was minimal at best. The wolf continued to come, its pace hardly slowed. The wolf's—*werewolf's*—sinewy body seemed to merely absorb the bullets.

Tony knew he needed to react, but his feet had grown roots. The wolf was closing the gap. Hard as he tried, Tony couldn't tear his eyes away from the imminent and assuredly grisly assault on the man in the black suit. A train wreck in the making.

The man made it halfway to Tony before the wolf cut him down. Its great momentum sent the two tumbling forward in a heap of arms and legs, fabric and fur. The man screamed once, brief and muffled, before the wolf tore out his throat with its jaws. An arc of blood painted a sickle on the gravel. When the wolf went back for seconds, it left the man nearly decapitated.

And for the first time, Tony wished he had shut off the headlights.

"Fuck this!" Tony broke from his trance and climbed behind the wheel of the Chevy. "And fuck Visili. Stupid bastard's on his own." He pulled the door shut and locked it, praying it would be enough to stop the savage beast, but knowing it wouldn't.

Tony turned the key.

The engine roared to life.

The wolf raised its head.

As it broke from shredding the dead man's face, the wolf turned toward Tony. Its snout curled. With what could very well have been a grin, the wolf licked its jowls and slowly rose on its back legs. When fully upright, the wolf topped out at nearly seven feet tall. With its back hunched, it began the thirty-yard trip that separated them.

By the time Tony reached for the gear shifter, the wolf was already on the hood. Tony bolted back in his seat. Remaining on two legs like no wolf should, the creature's eyes locked onto Tony's. It slowly stalked its way up the hood, its trance-like gaze never wavering. A snarl wrinkled its snout. Its entire muzzle, throat and chest were awash in a red sheen. At the windshield, the wolf nosed the glass directly in front of Tony, streaking it with foamy saliva and blood.

Drive, you asshole! You're a wheelman for fuck sake! Drive!

But Tony couldn't move. There was something in those grey eyes that froze him in his seat. Something wild, something familiar. And when the wolf's lips separated from gums, revealing post-meal teeth, Tony's bowels threatened to loosen.

It took that sensation to force him into action.

Once again, Tony reached for the gear shifter.

An explosion of glass threw him back against the seat.

When he looked up, panic gripped him in a clamp-like vice.

Two massive fur-covered fists protruded through holes in the windshield. When the fists opened up, the fingers grabbed the jagged edges of the glass, gripping it like it was made from nothing more than soft cotton. A second later, the windshield came away from the car without a fight.

When the warm night air rushed in through the gaping hole, it carried the coppery scent of blood.

Tony screamed.

The wolf cast aside the plate of glass like an empty beer can. Its strength was both impressive and terrifying. When the wolf turned back to Tony, its face was still scrunched up in a grin. It could smell his fear. Pink saliva dripped from its jowls in thin ribbons. Electric eyes bore down through storm clouds of grey fur.

A second scream broke free from Tony's throat.

He cowered further against the seat.

His frantic hands searched for something, anything with which to defend himself. But the car was void of any weaponry short of fast food napkins and...

Tony grabbed the cigarette case from the console. It was no match for a seven-foot muscle bound beast with sharpened stakes for teeth. But at least its corners were sharp.

The wolf leaned in through the opening where the windshield once was.

Tony, brandishing the silver case like a weapon, swung it through the air. A corner of the thin canister clipped the tip of the wolf's nose. It split the thick black hide, revealing pink underneath.

Within seconds, the wolf's expression changed. It reared back its head, shaking it as if trying to erase the infliction. A thin rivulet of smoke wafted from the wound. The wolf returned with eyes blazing. It bore its teeth even more than before. It elicited an angry growl.

Shit! Tony grasped the door handle. It wouldn't open.

When the wolf came through the opening the second

time, it brought more ferocity than before. A primitive roar brought about the unhinging of its jaws. Mouth agape, the wolf lunged at Tony.

When Tony swung the cigarette case around the second time, terror had zapped some of his resolve. Not to mention his strength. The effort was weak and missed the mark. The wolf caught Tony's hand in its mouth. Wrenching its head to the side, it took the cigarette case and Tony's hand with it.

Tony cried out in shock and excruciating agony. He brought a bloody stump back to his chest. The hand hadn't come off with the work of a gifted surgeon, but at the whim of a bloodthirsty animal. Jagged bone and ragged muscle replaced his hand. Streams of blood spurted from the exposed veins as he clutched the arm tightly. The pain was blinding, and it clouded Tony's vision.

The wolf hadn't come away unscathed. With its muzzle raised to the moon, a subtle, but visible lump jutted from its throat. The beast thrashed its head back and forth. It coughed and gagged as it fought to force the lump out. Or down.

Struggling to remain conscious, Tony came to a painful realization: his right hand, along with the silver cigarette case, now belonged to the wolf.

The wolf turned back, teeth gnashing. The lump in its throat was gone. But there was something peculiar about the way the wolf acted. Its snout twitched, as if it was about to sneeze. It seemed distracted. Its cold grey eyes, less focused.

This is it, Tony thought. Without a weapon, he couldn't fight. He tried and found that he couldn't shrink away any further. He jerked the door handle, now slick with blood, but it still refused to open.

The wolf leaned into the car, its snout only inches from Tony's face.

The cruelty in it suddenly softened. Its open jaw drifted slowly closed. The hatred in the wolf's eyes was abruptly replaced with fear.

The wolf retreated.

Its muscular legs began to quiver. Strange sounds erupted from its throat. Clutching its stomach, the abomination let out a long, painful cry before collapsing onto the hood of the idling Chevy.

Violent tremors shook the wolf's body. It convulsed and writhed in some phantom pain that Tony couldn't comprehend. Casting its head back in torment, the wolf flipped and flopped about like a fish on a dock. It whimpered softly as its body eventually came to rest.

When it was all over, the wolf lay sprawled across the hood on its side. One of its front paws hung lifeless over the edge, suspended in air.

A stillness overtook both the wolf and the night. The only sounds Tony heard were the low rumble of the Chevy's engine and his own labored breathing. With the threat momentarily neutralized, his body slumped into the seat, his ruined arm still clutched to his pounding chest. His shoulders sagged and his head hung. His chin rested on his chest.

Painful seconds ticked by. Then minutes.

It wasn't until he heard a slight scraping on the hood that Tony raised his eyes again. Whatever had happened to the wolf wasn't over, after all. Its massive body continued to shrink until it was reduced to a more familiar size. The head, once large with pointed ears on top, grew smaller, its shape more human-like. Long black fingernails shriveled away. Coarse grey fur melted, leaving behind only pink skin that seemed to roil and smolder from underneath.

Before Tony's very eyes, the mighty and terrifying wolf had transformed into a much smaller, yet still somewhat scary Visili Prek. His naked body emitted a light smoke. The stench of blood and seared flesh hung heavy in the air.

And the truth behind Visili's nature and why Tony was to tag along on this retrieval hit him like a sledgehammer to the face: the massacre was always the plan. Tony was simply a loose end in need of tying up in the process.

Two birds. One beastly and horrific stone.

Don't forget, Mr. Malone. I suggested killing you.

Shaking his head in disbelief, Tony lifted the door handle. This time when the door didn't open, he had time to investigate. Since a wolf—werewolf—was trying to eat his face earlier, Tony forgave himself for not remembering he had locked the door after climbing in.

After fixing the problem, Tony spilled out onto the ground. The tumble sent shockwaves through his arm that wouldn't ease no matter how hard he squeezed it. He lay on his back as the moon drifted behind a thin cloud, then reappeared just as effortlessly. His mouth felt like he had been dining on sand. He took measured breaths while wondering how much blood the human body could lose before succumbing. *That bastard Prek might just get his wish after all.*

Despite what it would mean, Tony couldn't help but chuckle at the irony.

The sound of a car door drew Tony's attention away from the night sky.

His chuckling ceased.

A pair of long, slender legs stepped from the rear passenger side of the SUV. As she came around the open door, Tony immediately recognized Ava even though the Chevy's headlights didn't reach that far. And as she stood in front of the SUV surveying the scene, it dawned on Tony who the men in the SUV were. They had met previously when he crossed them the day before. More specifically, when they had crossed him.

Ava's eyes found Tony on the ground beside the Chevy. She let them linger for an extended moment before making her way toward him. As she stepped into the flood of light between the vehicles, it soon became clear that she hadn't had a good thirty-six hours. Her hair was a mess, her white blouse dirty. A rip on one of the sleeves revealed a dark brown substance that was most assuredly dried blood.

Ava stopped briefly to look upon the remains of the man in the black suit. The one who had made a run for it. Corpse number three. Drawing her foot back, Ava kicked the man in the ribs. The impact made a sickening sound, like clubbing a meat piñata. Bending down, Ava retrieved the gun that lay in the dirt near the man's pulpy head.

Tony coughed. Iron-heavy blood filtered into his mouth and he spat it out.

Ava raised the gun, pointed it at Visili as she approached. "Glad he recognized me back there. For a second, I thought he wasn't going to."

Up close, Ava's face appeared to have some minor bruising around her chin. An angry red scrape sliced across one cheek. Her normally silky hair was dirty. Her ponytail resembled a haphazard array of unruly twine.

"You okay?" Tony asked.

Ava looked down at Tony, sprawled in the dirt, and laughed. "You in a position to help me if I wasn't? I mean, you did a real shit job looking out for me yesterday." She kept the gun trained on Visili, but her eyes scanned the wreckage of the Chevy. Its interior was awash in blood.

"Sorry." Tony licked at his cracked lips to no avail. His head felt so light, he feared he might float away. "If you can get me to a hospital, I might live long enough for your boyfriend to fire me."

"To be honest, I'm a little surprised that Vincent didn't have you killed. Loose ends, and all."

Tony looked up at the hood of the car where Visili's limp arm hung over the edge. "I'm not so sure he didn't try."

When Tony turned back to Ava, his heart sank. His blood turned to slush in his veins. Any thoughts of being helped to a hospital were forgotten. Ava no longer aimed the gun at Visili, but at Tony. Her expression showed no signs of reservation. There was no smile on her face. She found no pleasure in tying up loose ends.

Under different circumstances, Tony might have felt pity for her.

"I've asked him over and over," Ava said, sliding her long, manicured finger around the trigger, "why send a wolf when a gun is so much more efficient?"

The sound of the gunshot reached Tony's ears too late for him to hear it.

"The Company You Keep" was born from my second literary love, organized crime thrillers. I've always found both real and fictional gangsters fascinating. Nothing's personal. It's all business. Ordering a hit while they're getting ready for church on a Sunday morning. Fascinating.

I wrote the beginning of this story years ago, and it (along with a half-written gangster novel) has been sitting on my computer just waiting to be expanded upon. I like to think of them as marinating and not just collecting dust. Then an author friend suggested I try writing a werewolf story. I put the idea on the back burner, but it got my wheels turning. I kept coming back to the idea of a were-wolf story, but didn't have a story line. If I was going to write about one of the more iconic figures in horror, I wanted to offer a completely different take. Cue Tony Malone and the predicament he got himself into. A crime boss using a werewolf as a hit man? Well, hell, that seemed just far-fetched enough to be that different take on the genre that I was looking for.

The Bridge

By the light of a hunter's moon, Eva Marie Cobb shuffles her way down a dusty county road. The insides of her thighs are slick with fluid. There wasn't time to clean herself before. There isn't time for anything but this. A stray stone pierces the bottom of her bare foot, a reminder that not all pain can be so easily discarded.

She cradles a bundle tightly to her chest.

With the chill of the night air, her rapid breaths rise in evidence of her hurried pace. The shivering makes her muscles ache. It's October, yet her matted hair is damp with sweat. It clings to her face. The stench of a nearby skunk crosses her path. It mixes with her unsettled and empty belly and brings bile up the back of her throat. She retches, but quickly continues on. There is no time to waste.

She tosses another glance onto the moonlit road behind her. Her fear comes not from the dark, but from being discovered.

At the bridge, she puts one foot on the wood, worn by time and use, but hesitates. It is as if an invisible threshold confronts her, and once crossed, allows no turning back. She knows this, because she has crossed it twice before. Unsure if this will be the last, she can only hope. She takes a cautious second step, then a third. The cold planks sting the bottoms of her feet. She continues, one creak after the other, until she comes to the middle of the bridge. *The steel railing beckons her.*

The bundle sleeps soundly, without so much as a murmur, unaware of what's to come.

Through the gaps in the wooden planks, Eva can see the Boggy Creek flowing. She wonders where it leads. Where they end up. The babies her daddy keeps putting inside her.

She slowly makes her way to the railing.

She can remember a time before it all began. Before her mother passed and her father started looking at her the way he used to look at her mother. Before the bottle eroded his conscience. She remembers it still and holds the memory of that time more dearly than anything. Her memory is all that remains of the good man her father used to be. It is all that remains of love.

Standing at the railing, she looks down at the black water.

With a sudden gulp of air, she reaches across the top rail. The bundle hangs suspended over the water. Forty feet below, the rushing river awaits. The sound reaches her ears. She closes her eyes. Before she can change her mind, she releases the bundle. A tear falls as she waits, listening for that sound to signal the end of her ordeal. It takes only seconds for the splash to reach her.

She remains at the railing, second guessing long after the river has drowned out the tiny muffled cries. But there's no turning back. Not from this.

The echoes of a baby's cries follow her all the way home. They rip at her heart with scraggly claws. They scratch out the remaining vestiges of the self she used to be. That night, her sobs lull her to sleep as she prays for a redemption she doubts she deserves.

———

"That's pretty fucked up," Ronnie said, looking out the passenger window. I'd known Ronnie a long time and had never known him to mince words. "Killin' them babies like that. Seriously. Fucked. Up."

"Yeah, well," I said, my eyes on the winding road, "so is what her old man was doin' to her."

"How many they say she threw in the river?"

"At least three, as the legend goes."

"Son of a bitch."

He muttered that last sentence, but the sentiment was easy to unpack. I'd had more or less the same reaction upon hearing the story of the Crybaby Bridge for the first time. Disbelief with a hearty helping of disgust. "Yeah," I said. "Son of a bitch."

If Alderson Road saw a car an hour, especially after dark, I would be surprised. More likely, it didn't see any. There wasn't much to see or do out this way. Unless, of course, mile after mile of flat open range and cows were your thing. They weren't mine. We did, however, have a reason for our trip. Something we wanted to see. Something that probably failed to make most peoples' bucket lists.

The pavement was old, sun-bleached to a light grey and cracked. It carried us around a hairpin turn. When the Buick's headlights caught back up with the road, they shed light on an ancient relic sitting dormant up ahead. I let up on the gas and pulled off the road. On a gravel patch just short of the bridge, I put the car in park. Having been over the Alderson bridge a couple dozen times by truck, I wanted to walk the rest of the way. My trips to McAlester, where I would occasionally drop off feed for Old Man Rennick, brought me through the area. But this was the first time I had been on the bridge at night. I wanted to ease up to it.

A warm breeze greeted me as I climbed out of the car and gently shut the door.

The legend of the Alderson Road Bridge was well known to those in the surrounding counties. The story of babies crying in the night had long ago established itself in the area's folklore. From the old drunks teetering on barstools, to the young kids whose parents wouldn't allow talk of that sort at the dinner table, everyone knew someone who knew someone who had heard the cries first hand. And even though there were skeptics, the stories of ghosts kept most God-fearing folk away. Most, that is, but not all. Two specific groups were naturally inclined to venture out to the bridge after dark: testosterone-fueled teenage boys wanting to prove they had balls; and alcohol-fueled men trying to prove they hadn't lost theirs.

We were among the latter.

It had been one of those nights where, as each hour ticked by, you just knew you were going to end up spending the whole evening with your buddies at the bar before eventually staggering home to your solitary existence. Meaning, you'd struck out with every woman you approached. And that included Miss Ginger Lynn Beecher, who no one ever struck out with. Earlier that night, I'd made my pitch too late. Miss Beecher had already chosen some unfortunate sad sack to screw her loneliness away, if only for one evening. Striking out with the surest thing in town made me sadder than normal. And pathetic.

"You know you're too damn ugly to take home to *my* mama," Ronnie said as we left my Buick Skylark on the shoulder and started up the pavement in the dark. The trip out had been spur of the moment, leaving us less than prepared for exploration. The moon would have to light the way. Ronnie carried the remainder of a 12-pack by the open end. It wasn't too heavy, which spoke to our evening since leaving the bar. As for Nelson, we left him passed out in the back seat, an early, if not ungracious, end to his Saturday night.

"Yeah, but the fact you still live with your mama says a lot about your standards."

"I know, right?"

Then we laughed. We laughed because it was funny. We laughed because it was true. Mostly we laughed to cover up how pathetic and sad our lives were.

The closer we got to the bridge, the further its ironwork stretched into the night. Like the bare bones of a high-rise, the network of crossbeams towered above the overgrown brush that surrounded the bridge. Looking at it from below, their interconnecting design cut the starlit sky into geometric shapes.

At the bridge's edge, old pavement gave way to even older wood planking. You could wedge a beer can in the gaps between the thick boards, and the threat of a forty-foot drop promised to do a number on my stomach. I willed the drunken butterflies to settle and continued walking.

The hollow sound of our work boots echoed in the space below. Each footfall further announced our arrival. As we walked in silence, thoughts of what brought us out here entered my mind. I imagine the same could be said for Ronnie.

Once we'd reached the middle of the bridge, I made my way to the steel railing. Its black paint was flaking, losing its battle with rust. I could hear the light trickling of water.

I looked over the side.

Any other time of year, the Boggy Creek would be sweeping through the area at a decent clip. But now it only dribbled, its payload diminished by a dry plains summer. I could faintly hear the water, but couldn't see a damn thing.

The stream itself was cloaked in darkness. The moon had dipped behind a clump of clouds, and I hoped the loss of light was only temporary. Being out here at night was creepy enough. But with no light…

"You bring a flashlight?" Ronnie asked, stepping up beside me.

My mouth was dry and in need of a beer. "Done told you I didn't."

"Shit." Ronnie's silhouette scratched his chin. "That's right."

We lingered for several minutes, leaning over the railing. We swayed despite the lack of a breeze, which I chalked up to too many Coors Lights. It was the same reason my stomach sloshed when I walked.

With the urban legend front and center in my mind, I listened intently for any sounds that didn't belong in the setting. It was as if I'd been put on this Earth for the single purpose of proving the legend either real or fake. It was a weighty job. I was all too happy to do it, though. I'd all but guaranteed Ronnie we would hear the crying baby just to get him to come along.

But after several minutes, I hadn't heard anything. And I don't think Ronnie had either, or he would have said so.

Ronnie spit over the side and watched it until it disappeared. "I don't hear nothin'."

I kicked the toe plate of the railing, sending a metallic clang out into the night. "Me, neither," I admitted. The air deflated from my shoulders. I wasn't sure whether to be relieved or disappointed. Would not hearing a crying baby debunk the myth? Maybe, but probably not. Excuses would be made and we'd have to do it all over again.

I crouched and grabbed a seat on the bridge, leaning my back against the railing. "Maybe it just takes a while," I said. "Hand me a beer. We got nowhere to be."

It wasn't until Ronnie was taking a piss over the side two beers later that I got the first sense we weren't wasting our time.

"Sum bitch!" Ronnie hastily started fumbling with himself.

I started laughing. "What's wrong ol' buddy? You get something caught there?"

"You hear that?" he asked, ignoring my question and completely robbing me of a well-timed punch line.

I climbed to my feet and peered over the railing. The moon was peeking out from behind the clouds, so I could see the shimmering water meander its way along the banks. The gentle babbling drifted up to my ears. I didn't think that was the sound Ronnie was talking about. "Hear what?"

"It was— fuck's sake, you really didn't hear it?" The more anxious Ronnie grew, the softer his voice got. It was like his adrenaline was squandering all his energy.

From a good forty feet above, I searched the rocks and water below. I was usually a good judge of when Ronnie was bullshitting me and when he wasn't. This time, I wasn't sure, but I felt myself giving him the benefit of the doubt. It was possible he simply *thought* he heard something. Especially with the alcohol flowing through him.

Because I didn't hear a damn thing.

I gave Ronnie a little shove to the side. "You fuckin' with me, dude?"

"Nah, man," Ronnie said, using the railing to maintain his balance. "Dead serious. It came from down there somewhere." Ronnie pointed to the shadowy space below the bridge where the moonlight wasn't allowed. It was a rather expansive area. He did nothing to narrow it down for me.

"Okay, then," I said. "Give me something to go on. What did it sound like?"

"It sounded like—" Ronnie's mouth clamped shut. He leaned dangerously far over the railing, wide eyed. "There! Did you hear it?"

Sonofabitch.

A knot formed in my stomach.

I heard it that time, and tiny hairs stood on the back of my neck. The soft, muffled cries of a baby drifted up from somewhere beneath us. They were faint at first, but grew in volume with each passing second. We stood at the railing, paralyzed, waiting for a gust of wind or some other explanation to present itself. But nothing did. As minutes passed, more cries joined the first until it sounded like the wails were coming from more than one baby.

At least three, as the legend goes.

I looked to Ronnie, who was leaning way too far over the railing for his condition. I envisioned him going ass over teakettle. I wasn't prepared for a swim. I grabbed my buddy by the waistband of his jeans and hauled him back over the top rail.

As soon as Ronnie's boots hit the bridge, he took a few steps back. He put his hands to his head and ran his fingers through his hair. His eyes could have doubled as headlights.

"Look," I said. "I know the water's low right now. Doesn't mean I wanna fish your ass outta that river. Not tonight."

But Ronnie was listening to me as much as a rebellious teenager listens to an overbearing parent. To his ears, squawks and muted trombones replaced my voice. His mind was elsewhere. His face was ashen. It was as if he'd seen a...

I erased the thought from my mind, and joined Ronnie in the middle of the bridge. Mounting adrenalin kept me from returning to the railing. More cries reached my ears, and that was the first time I noticed how fast my heart was beating. I grabbed a fresh beer from the carton. I started pacing the bridge, though never straying too far from Ronnie.

"So, what are you thinking?"

Ronnie looked at me as if I'd spoken with a foreign tongue. His furrowed brow left nothing to the imagination, his scowl nothing to interpret. I wasn't sure he was going to answer until his mouth started forming the words. Even then, he shed as much light on the situation as a flashlight with dead batteries.

"I don't know." Ronnie rubbed his temple as he spoke. His glassy eyes patrolled the length of the bridge as if he expected company at any moment. I shot a glance myself. Admittedly, if a car had come by right then, I wouldn't have minded. "But by God, I heard something. And it came from down there."

Ronnie pointed at the wooden planks below our feet, but I knew what he meant.

While I didn't share Ronnie's certainty, I was having the same thoughts. "Pretty sure I heard it, too." I paused for a moment, my ear trained on the darkness. But the night was still. The cries had stopped. At one point, I had to remind myself to breathe. "But I ain't hearin' it now. Maybe the wind? An animal of some sort."

Ronnie turned to me. The little bit of moonlight peeking through the clouds revealed a look I'd come to know well over our nearly twenty-year friendship: he wasn't buying what I was selling. If he needed more reason to doubt my theories, fate came along, its timing never more perfect.

The sound billowed up again.

It was louder.

This time there was no question. It wasn't the wind, and it sure as shit wasn't an animal.

It was a baby. A crying baby.

Ho-ly shit.

Ronnie and I exchanged a look. Alarm replaced the earlier curiosity in his eyes. I'm sure the same could have been said of my own, because that's exactly how I felt: afraid. I had never before crossed paths with the supernatural. I always questioned it, even doubted. But, I was no longer a skeptic. Nor were my thoughts tainted by alcohol.

I was stone cold sober. And I believed.

"So…" I took a few seconds before continuing. My imagination was dealing out possible explanations like a Vegas croupier. My mind was the virgin gambler, struggling to keep up. Ultimately, I decided to put some of the more reasonable explanations out there for discussion. "Seems to me there are three possible explanations."

The cries continued, though their volume lessened by a degree.

Ronnie stared at me, ignoring the sound. With his thumb pressed firmly against his temple, he vigorously rubbed his forehead with the other four fingers.

"Explanation number one," I continued. "We're just hearing things."

Ronnie gave me that look a second time. "Both of us?"

I set my beer down in the middle of the bridge, too anxious to drink.

"Hey, I said these were *possible* explanations, not probable." The way Ronnie worked the inside of his mouth, I could tell this explanation sounded as lame to him as it had when it first entered my mind. But that was okay. Nothing else, the possibility of our imaginations run amok needed to be ruled out.

"Number two." I used my fingers to help count. "The

stories are real, and we're dealing with an honest to goodness ghost." Even as I spoke the words, I was sure of Ronnie's reaction.

I was wrong.

Ronnie stared at me, unblinking, urging me on. The word "ghost" hadn't even fazed him.

"You mean ghosts."

I nodded. "You're right," I said. "The legend says there was more than one baby."

"You said three."

"Something like that." I picked up my beer, took a long swallow and set it back down. "Possibility number three, it's a natural occurrence. An animal or the wind. Though I'll admit, neither seems likely. Those cries sound pretty damn much like a human baby."

"Exactly. Explanation number four," Ronnie said. "It sounds like a real baby because it *is* a real fuckin' baby."

"Shit." My reaction was immediate, not to mention dismissive. "How the hell could a baby get down there?"

Ronnie's arms flew out to his sides. "I don't know, man." His face contorted with uncertainty. "How the hell could a father be so messed up?"

Ronnie's argument caught me off guard, and I glanced over at the railing. The possibility of the cries coming from an actual baby, compared to the ones I'd come up with, seemed the least likely explanation. But, it was certainly the most plausible. What could make the sound of a crying baby better than an actual baby?

"Should I check it out?" Ronnie asked. "I mean, don't we have to? Just to be sure?"

I looked back at my friend of many years. Something about him seemed different. Unfamiliar. I blamed it on the fact that we were knee deep in a situation unique to anything we'd experienced before. The most excitement we ever came across was the occasional bar fight. A game of pool gone bad, or somebody grabbing the ass of someone they shouldn't have. Paranormal investigators, we were not. "I don't know, Sherlock. Should we?"

The debate was tabled when absolute silence returned. The sounds of babies' cries retreated, replaced with a hushed sense of calm.

We shuffled to the rail and peered over the side. Moonlight glistened like fine China on the stream flowing up, over, and through the rocks. The brush along the banks swayed in a gentle breeze. Any other time, it would have been a tranquil, if not calming, scene.

Ronnie looked at me, eyebrows cocked. He wore mischief on his face like a mask. "What about teenagers? You know, screwin' around down there?"

My shoulders did a quick up and down. "Explanation number five? I don't know, could be." I didn't see any other cars around, but it was possible. I was up for the sounds coming from anything but a real baby or the spirits of ones that used to be.

"Only one way to find out." Ronnie playfully punched me in the shoulder. "Come on, shithead."

I felt myself nodding, though my heart was backpedaling. I was never big on confrontation, even with teenagers half my age. It was a trait held over from when I *was* a teenager. And as remote as it was, there was still the possibility that we were dealing with a wild animal. A very large, wounded animal even. And who the hell wants to run into one of those under a dark bridge in the middle of the night armed with little more than a half empty can of cheap beer? Hiking down to the water to investigate where the cries might be coming from was never part of the evening's discussion.

Though I tried to come up with a reasonable excuse not to follow, there really was none. I had no choice.

After scrutinizing both inclines, we decided the north-west downslope would be the easiest path of descent. Its terrain was steep and rocky, but bathed in moonlight. At least we'd be able to see where the hell we were going. We had no idea what the other side was like. It was fully engulfed in the bridge's shadow, leaving too much to the imagination. And in my imagination, death lived on that shadowy downslope.

Ronnie started down first, and I let him, stalling long enough to light up a borrowed cigarette. Knowing Ronnie and how well he knew me, I'm sure he read between the lines. But he didn't say anything. I hadn't smoked in years. It just seemed like a good time to pick the habit back up. Suddenly, I wasn't so anxious to prove myself anymore. Who cared if I still had balls? Not to mention this was a shitty way to prove it. Blowing out a plume of smoke, I downed the last of my beer before tossing the can and following in Ronnie's footsteps.

The rocks were large and jagged. This made them both dangerous and easy to negotiate. There were plenty of footholds when I needed them. Ambitious weeds snaked through the voids between the rocks, sprouting wherever space allowed. I tried not to think about what else might be snaking around and in between, but wasn't entirely successful. My punishment for being an Animal Planet junkie with a vivid imagination.

It took a good three or four minutes and one deeply bruised shin to navigate my way down to the river's edge. Once there, the soft grassy bank was a welcome change of pace. But it didn't come without its perils. Much of the grass along the bank was tall and falling over under its own weight. This overgrowth blurred the line between land and water and shrouded the bank's edge in mystery. Especially at night. Footing was treacherous. Every step along the overgrown bank that came up dry felt like a victory.

I found the world below the bridge vastly different than the world above it. The world below was alive. Running water gurgled along its journey. The buzz of crickets and mayfly wings reminded me I was treading on their territory. The air was thick and humid, causing sweat to collect on my forehead.

The bridge loomed larger and more imposing from down below. It's steel girders bore the weight of graffiti. I could see splashes of color, but the lack of light made the words difficult to read. I imagined the usual artistic fare: so and so loves so and so; class of current year rules; Justin Bieber sucks. I made out Ronnie's silhouette thirty yards upstream and carefully started in his direction.

Ronnie was already on the other side. Reaching him meant I had to cross underneath the bridge. Stepping into its shadowy bowels turned a relatively moonlit night into a nearly pitch-black void. I didn't see the clump of cattails until they slapped me across the face. I didn't know what was brushing against my arms. Each step was cautious and placed with care, while still trying to speed up my pace. I couldn't exit the darkness fast enough. Emerging on the other side felt like a rebirth. I breathed a little easier. My eyes took a moment to adjust.

The sound of crickets greeted me.

This seemed like as good a place as any to relieve my bladder's burden. Taking one last drag off my cigarette, I dropped it into the grass. I used the toe of my boot to grind it out. Unzipping my fly, I proceeded to douse it, removing any question of igniting a potential forest fire.

From somewhere downstream, a shout of surprise ripped through the night. My breath caught in my throat.

My heart rate peaked. I zipped my fly and looked for Ronnie's silhouette. When I found it, he was doubled over. I began high stepping through the thick brush, hidden hazards be damned. A twisted ankle awaited me somewhere along the way, I was sure.

"Ronnie!" Adrenaline powered me along the river bank. Had something happened? Had he found something? A baby? These and a hundred other thoughts ran through my mind. "Hey, man! You alright?"

When I finally drew up beside him, it wasn't the scene I'd expected to find. Ronnie stood upright, shaking his head and mumbling profanity. Other than that, he seemed relatively unharmed. He just looked pissed.

"Dude!" I said, trying to catch my breath. "What the hell happened?"

Ronnie looked down at his jeans. Even in the murky light I could see that his right pant leg was a dark blue, almost black, from the knee down.

"Missed the edge of the bank." Ronnie lifted his foot and shook it. "Water's damn cold," he said. "And deeper than it looks."

I took a quick look around. No babies. No teenagers. Not even a wild animal. I shook my head, unsure whether to be relieved or irritated that a soggy leg was all that had befallen my friend. Ultimately, I settled somewhere in between, leaning more toward relief. But that didn't let him off the hook.

"Seriously, man? That's what the commotion was about?" I used my shirtsleeve to wipe away the sweat running down my forehead.

Ronnie just looked at me like the kid who doesn't get it when someone tries to impart wisdom. "Damn cold," he reiterated. He followed up with a shrug.

I turned away and swatted something that had been tickling the back of my neck.

Standing in the mire along the Boggy Creek, my thoughts turned to what might have been: an evening spent with Ginger Lynn Beecher. I could have been somewhere a hell of a lot nicer, doing something a hell of a lot more fun with someone a hell of a lot more attractive. Instead, my ass was hanging out under a bridge, battling blood-sucking insects with my dipshit friend, knowing full well a hangover awaited me in the morning. Talk about missed opportunities.

If only I had shown up at the bar ten minutes sooner…

When Ronnie gasped, I had forgotten why we were even down by the creek. When he grabbed my arm and jerked on it, I let out an exhaustive sigh.

"Dude." I turned to him, holding back my growing irritation. "Stop with the boy who cried wolf bull—"

Ronnie's eyes were wide. His jaw hung like a sprung trapdoor. He dropped to a crouched position, pulling me down into the brush alongside him. In doing so, my foot missed the edge of the bank, finding water instead of land. Pulling it back, I started to protest.

Ronnie jammed his finger against his lips. "Shh!" But ultimately, it was his scowl that shushed me. He turned and aimed that scowl to the bridge above. He directed my attention to it with a nod.

When I saw it, I drew in a sharp breath.

More specifically, when I saw *her*.

A young woman, her body transparent as if fashioned from nothing but the moon's rays, stood at the railing in the center of the bridge. The lack of pigment in her gown allowed the treetops behind her to show through. Her hair clung to her head, unmoved by the gentle breeze. Her face was a hybrid of fear and sorrow. She cradled a swaddled bundle in her arms.

There was little doubt what was inside.

I remained crouched in the brush, transfixed, unable to look away. There was a chance I was being bitten by all manner of insects. A good chance. But if I was, I didn't notice. A colony of fire ants marching up my pant leg couldn't have torn my eyes from the young woman.

"How long ago was this?" Ronnie kept his voice above a whisper, but below the crickets. "You know, this thing with the girl and the babies?"

"Long time." I kept my voice just as low. "1800s, I'd guess."

"Well, she looks pretty damn good for her age."

And he was right. From where I stood, the woman appeared not only young, but striking. She couldn't have been more than sixteen, seventeen years old, and already her beauty was evident. Her long, light colored-hair, her soft features. Slightly taller than most. Other than the old-fashioned gown, she could have passed for a typical high schooler from any one of the neighboring towns. Only instead of looking carefree and jovial like most young women her age, this young woman's posture carried the weight of the world in it.

"Is she a..." I let the sentence die. I couldn't bring myself to say the "g word." Not in her presence, and that alone added to the mystery.

When our eyes met a moment later, Ronnie had no such problem. "Ghost?" Without waiting for a response, his gaze returned to the railing. Mine followed. I couldn't take my eyes off of the apparition for more than a few seconds. It was an extraordinary sight, and my heartrate responded accordingly.

A second after looking up, though, I wished I hadn't.

The young woman no longer hugged the bundle to her chest. She no longer cradled it in her arms. Those thin arms were now outstretched. The bundle hung suspended over the deepest part of the river. I sucked in air, poised to shout. But I reacted too late, and the scream died before it could escape.

It took the bundle all of two seconds to hit the water. At least I think it hit the water. The moonlight shimmering on the stream's surface could have played tricks on my eyes. Still, my ears were working just fine. And I didn't hear a sound.

"Did…" Ronnie's voice cracked. "Did you see that?"

I nodded, wanting to speak, but somehow unable to.

The same couldn't be said for Ronnie. "Not even a splash," he said. "It just…disappeared."

My focus remained squarely on the spot where the bundle should have hit, waiting for a splash that would never come. How was it even possible? It wasn't. Not for any scenario other than the obvious: it had been an apparition. Plain and simple. And that meant the stories were true. The Alderson Road Bridge had its very own ghost.

It wasn't until I looked up and saw that the young woman was gone that my voice recovered.

"Holy shit, Ronnie!" It wasn't profound, but it was the best I could offer at the time. Strangely enough, it relayed my sentiments perfectly. I grabbed my friend by the shoulders, about to follow up with something more intelligent, when a voice from above stole the moment.

"Hey, what are you guys doin' down there?" It was Nelson, raised from his backseat slumber. "You two need some privacy? I can go back to the car."

I rose up from the weeds and brushed off my pants, ignoring Nelson's joke. "Do you see her?"

The tip of Nelson's cigarette blazed orange before he

pulled the stick from his mouth. He tilted his head back and a volcano of smoke erupted from it. "See who?" he asked, looking from side to side.

"The girl!" My voice sounded like a bullhorn in the night. I felt more than a little self-conscious.

Nelson looked around again. He threw his hands up. "Ain't no girl up here, man."

And then I heard it, softly at first, but growing louder. The panicked wails of an infant.

My blood froze.

The hairs on my arms stood up.

I looked to Ronnie for his thoughts. He was busy looking to me for mine. When he started shaking his head, I knew what was coming. I felt the same way.

"I'm out." And Ronnie turned away.

Navigating up the embankment took a surprisingly shorter amount of time than going down. Maybe our incentive was more sharply defined the second time. The pace of my heartbeat alone propelled me up the hill, knees and shins be damned. I was ready to call it a night. Not to mention a little saddened by what I'd seen. Hearing about the young woman tossing her babies into the river and seeing it firsthand were two completely different things. I didn't know if I'd ever get the image out of my mind. It wouldn't be soon. Of that I was certain.

We arrived at the top to find the scene just as Nelson had described. He stood alone in the middle of the bridge. The young woman was gone.

After gathering our empty beer cans, the three of us walked the shoulder of the road back to my car in silence. Gravel crunched beneath our feet as we put the bridge farther behind us with every step. The wind was picking up. Leaves rustled in the treetops. The air had turned noticeably cooler since we had arrived. It wouldn't be long before summer would be over and rain would once again swell the Boggy Creek.

At some point, the woeful cries of a baby were silenced by distance. None of us missed them. None of us looked back.

With our empties stowed in the trunk, everyone assumed their original positions in the car. I cranked the Buick's steering wheel hard to the left and performed a U-turn in the middle of Alderson Road. The mood inside the car was somber. The radio played an upbeat Kenny Chesney song about girls and beer and sand, but the volume was low. I don't think anyone paid any attention. I pointed the headlights toward town, putting the bridge and its spirits behind us.

"I don't know, fellas. That's a pretty wild story." From the backseat, Nelson drew on his cigarette, blew smoke out the window and passed judgment. "I mean, I heard the cries, too. But, actually seeing the girl do it? I don't know."

By the glow of the Buick's dashboard, Ronnie and I exchanged a look. We may not have believed it either had we both not been there to witness it. We knew what we saw. For the rest of our lives there would be somebody there to say, "you weren't just seeing things. You aren't crazy."

"Can't get the image out of my head." Ronnie's voice was subdued. He sounded defeated, as if the answer to the grand question still eluded him. "How does someone hold their baby out over the water like that and just fuckin' let go? I don't care who the daddy is."

I could only shake my head and try to keep my eyes on the road. It was tough. My focus was elsewhere. Even knowing the backstory, watching the urban legend play out before my eyes was unsettling to say the least. The odds of me getting any sleep that night were a long shot at best.

Nelson's hand grabbed my shoulder. "What the hell?" His breath smelled of cigarettes and stale beer. But something in his voice caused me to sit up straighter, more alert. I could see him in the rearview mirror. His brow was wrinkled; his eyes were squinted and trained on the road ahead. Leaning forward, Nelson positioned himself between Ronnie and me and pointed through the windshield. "Guys, look!"

When I did, I sucked in air and held it, afraid to breathe. No one made a sound. I let up on the gas and the car started to slow. We focused solely on the figure entering the cusp of the Buick's headlights.

A young woman, dressed in a short, white gown, walked along the side of the road. She was heading right toward us. If the shine of the headlights bothered her, she didn't show it. Her pace was hurried. Determination and purpose were her guides. Her feet were bare.

And in her arms she carried a swaddled blanket.

I slammed on the brakes. The Buick came to a screeching halt in the middle of the road. The dust of three weeks without rain billowed up, filling the twin beams of light. The woman didn't falter. Her eyes remained forward, just not on us.

I acted without thought or plan. With a deep breath and Ronnie in my ear asking what the hell I was doing, I threw open the car door and climbed out.

The young woman was steadfast. Even as I made my way around the back of the car, she continued on. If she saw me, her face didn't register the fact. Her feet kicked up tiny clouds of dust as she passed beyond the headlights' reach. From the corner of my eye, I saw both Ronnie and Nelson's heads turn as she passed the passenger side door. So close, they could have reached out and touched her.

Keeping within arms-length of the Buick, I moved

onto the gravel shoulder and into the young woman's path. Even from ten feet away, her eyes didn't find me. It was as if I was the one breaking the laws of reality, not her. As she neared the rear of the car, I heard the creak of a door.

"Dude!" Ronnie's brief shout was meant to call me back.

It didn't work. I couldn't have turned back if I'd wanted to. My feet had grown roots in the pavement.

Only a few steps separated us.

I could make out her features. Her eyes never turned upward. She simply stared at the ground ahead. A storm of fear and sadness swirled in the depths of her expression. Tears trailed down her cheeks, cutting paths through dirt and filth.

And still, it was as if I wasn't even there. I took a deep breath as she closed in, unsure what to expect once contact was made.

Two more steps.

One step.

I drew my hands up over my eyes, shielding them from the flash of bright light. A vacuum sucked the breath from my throat. My skin sizzled as an electric current surged through me. The muscles in my back seized. My entire body went rigid. My knees found gravel.

When I dared peek out from behind my hands, my world had changed. I no longer stood in the middle of Alderson Road. I was now somewhere else. Somewhere completely and utterly foreign…

The young woman lays on a bed of straw, but she doesn't sleep. She doesn't rest. Her soiled white dress is hiked up over a slightly protruding stomach, her chest heaves violently. Her knees are up and slightly open. Damp strands of long, unkempt hair cling to her face. With a hand over her mouth, she stifles a scream.

An older woman with darker skin and lesser clothing kneels beside the girl. She draws a damp cloth across her forehead. The woman's touch is gentle, but her voice is harsh. Somehow, I understand that it needs to be.

Somewhere in a dark corner of the barn, a cow mews.

"This baby's not safe for this God-less world, child."

The young woman casts her head backward. Clenched lips spit a string of unintelligible words through rapid breaths.

The older woman dips the cloth into a bucket of water. Pulling it back out, she wrings off the excess. "You know it won't have a fair shake. Not in this town. Not in this house." The older woman once again puts the cloth to the young woman's forehead.

A stifled scream escapes the young woman's throat. Others follow, but she grits her teeth and holds them back. Only spittle spews forth. She draws her arms up and around her belly. Each labored breath now comes through a sob. Tears run down her face.

"Think of it, child. Think of the man it'll grow into under this roof. The things it'll learn. And if it's a girl…" The woman let the sentence trail off. "You must break the cycle."

"What then?" The young woman forces the words through labored breaths. "What can I do?"

The older woman drops the cloth into the bucket of water. "There is something, child." The older woman lays a hand on the girl's stomach, crosses her heart with the other. "But musn't no one see you. They's eyes all around, and if they catch you… But dear child, you must go. You must get to the bridge."

A gasp escapes my lips. It draws unwanted attention. The younger woman is too busy to notice, but the older woman turns burning, angry eyes toward me.

Ice forms in my blood. I shiver.

The older woman mumbles something in a foreign tongue before dismissing me with a sweep of her hand. "Be gone, devil!"

My eyes shot open. Air filled my lungs, and I gulped it like I'd been deprived for some time. Like I'd been underwater. The warm energy that had coursed through my body was gone. Cold sweat and goose bumps covered my arms. I knelt on the shoulder of Alderson Road, the Buick idling beside me.

"Holy shit!" Ronnie and Nelson flanked my sides, each offering a hand. I took them up on their offer and got to my feet. The three of us turned to watch the young woman continue on her journey. The moonlight illuminated her white gown against the backdrop of night. The further away she got, the less visible she became.

"Is that her?" Nelson asked. "Is that the crazy bitch who killed her babies?"

"Hey!" I reacted without thinking. Grabbing Nelson's jacket, I unleashed with the first thought that came to mind. "Don't call her that!"

"Whoa, whoa, whoa!" Ronnie put a hand my shoulder and another on my chest. "Alright, man. It's cool."

I let out a deep exhale. I let go of my friend's jacket. Turning to Ronnie, I was met with a concerned stare. My eyes searched his, wishing I could explain. Somehow, I think he knew.

"Should we follow her?" Nelson asked, seemingly unfazed by the sudden reproach.

I looked down the road. The young woman was but a blip of white in the distance.

"No," I said, shaking my head. I rubbed my hands over my arms, trying to work some warmth into them. "Let her go."

"Okay, fellas," Ronnie said. He gave me another once

over, still taking inventory of my faculties. "It's been a long ass night. Let's get the hell outta here, yeah?"

Sitting behind the wheel, I checked the rearview for one last glimpse of the young woman. She was gone.

"Got one left." Nelson shook the near empty carton. The sound of a lone beer can rolling around the cardboard box was a lonely one. "Who wants it?"

I shook my head, my thoughts elsewhere. "You go ahead. I'm good." And as I drove the deserted country road toward town, I wondered how I would feel the next time I came this way on a delivery. *If* I came this way again. The only thing I knew for sure was that the sun would be up if I did. I wouldn't be returning at night. I doubted I'd ever see the young woman again. The thought both relieved and saddened me.

———

"The Bridge" is based on an urban legend supposedly originating in Alderson, Ok. It is said that a young woman, repeatedly raped and impregnated by her father, would take the newborns to the bridge and toss them into the river. While researching this mythology, I was surprised to find that there is an entire sub-genre of urban legends that has come to be known as the "crybaby bridge." It seems every state in the nation has these bridges, with most having more than one. Whether the stories revolve around young women tossing their babies into the river, or murdered young lovers whose car had broken down somewhere along its span, there is probably a bridge swirling in legend somewhere not too far from where you live. I encourage you to check one out for yourself. (And if you're in Ohio, let me know. I'd love to tag along!)

No Saints Here

There is nothing particularly special about the panties; burgundy satin with frilly white lace along the edges. A tiny white bow sits in the center of the waistband. The under-garment could have been purchased at any number of upscale clothing stores or intimate apparel outlets. But it is not the fashion forwardness of the panties that interests Clancy. It is the fragrant aroma of woman that makes him bury his face in the clump of silky fabric. He breathes in her scent as if the woman herself were hidden deep inside the folds. She has spent the last week and a half strutting half-naked through the house while Clancy has struggled to maintain professionalism. All he can think about is throwing her on her bed and having his way with her. Maybe on the bathroom floor. Maybe the shower.

Hell, why not the walk-in closet he just remodeled for her? It is, after all, as large as his entire bedroom, with just as much floor space.

Clancy imagines all the ways he would take her on that floor space.

The word "integrity" may be printed on the side of his

work truck, listed alongside other business-friendly traits Clancy promotes and usually tries to live up to. But every man has his vice. Clancy's vice is exploring his clients' personal belongings at each remodeling site. Sometimes it is their medicine cabinets; sometimes their dresser drawers. This time just happened to be the white wicker clothes hamper sitting in the corner of her bedroom. It's not entirely Clancy's fault. People shouldn't let strange men roam their homes unattended.

His work is done, the closet is finished, but Clancy doesn't want to part with his new find just yet. He balls up the panties and slips them into the front of his carpenter khakis. He has seen the size of her clothing collection. He doubts she'll miss this one undergarment. The silky cloth feels good against his skin, and he is glad he stopped wearing underwear a while back.

Clancy gives the newly remodeled closet one last look, then makes his way to the bed. He sweeps his hand across the rumpled sheets. He isn't sure which side of the bed is hers, so he uses his imagination. He closes his eyes and sees her laying there, naked and beckoning. There is no question she wants him. When his heart rate starts to elevate and his mouth goes dry, Clancy opens his eyes, forcing the image from his mind. He switches off the light and exits the master bedroom.

As he descends the curved staircase with the wrought iron spindles, Clancy can hear the two of them talking in the kitchen. Matt and Chloe. Husband and wife. The Andersons. Adjusting his crotch to make sure the wadded undergarment bulges in just the right place, Clancy strolls into the couple's gourmet kitchen. He sets his clipboard on the granite countertop and pulls out a stool from the island. Plopping down, he waits for the couple to finish their conversation.

Like he's seen her do a hundred times in the past ten days, the wife stands with her hands on her hips, thrusting her chest out while she talks. She brandishes it like a weapon. And just like the other hundred times, Clancy is immediately enthralled. Not because of anything the woman says, but because it is one hell of a chest.

"The name and number are on the pad," she tells her husband. She points to a pink, flower-shaped Post-It pad sitting on the countertop beside Clancy. "The website says not to count on cell service, so if you can't get ahold of me..." She lets the sentence die as if finishing it would be pointless.

"Goin' on a trip?" Clancy asks. He hands the clipboard with his work order and invoice to the husband, but his eyes never leave the aforementioned chest.

"Sorta." The wife is as bubbly as Clancy has ever seen her. "I won a weekend at a spa over by Montgomery."

"Still not sure how," the husband says, looking over Clancy's invoice. "You don't even listen to that radio station."

"My God, Mr. Jealous here! You go on your hunting trips. Don't I deserve some me time once in a while?" The wife punctuates her question with a light finger tap to the end of her husband's nose. She twirls and slinks over to the refrigerator. When she pulls open the set of stainless-steel doors and bends over to retrieve something from a bottom shelf, she offers Clancy quite the view. Her white denim capris show no signs of panty lines. The hem of her blouse rides up, and the gap between it and the top of her pants reveals a patch of smooth, tanned skin.

Clancy takes in the view for only so long. The husband, after all, stands only a few feet away, and Clancy has learned over the years not to draw too much attention to himself. She is dragging it out, though, the tease. They both know it doesn't take that long to get something out of the fridge.

"Two whole days of pampering," the wife says, closing the refrigerator door. She returns to the island with a small bottle of green liquid. When she shakes it, everything else shakes, too. "Massage. Mani Pedi. Little bit of hot yoga."

"Don't tell my wife," Clancy says, producing a smile. "She'd jump all over an opportunity like that." He is full of shit, of course. His wife wouldn't jump at the opportunity, mainly because he doesn't have one. If either of the Andersons had asked why he wasn't wearing a ring, he would have had an answer ready for them: he simply didn't like to wear it while he worked for fear of damaging it. But they didn't ask.

"Well," says the husband, taking hold of the pen that is attached to the clipboard, "everything looks good here."

It sure does. Clancy eyes the wife's full blouse one last time before rising. *It sure as hell does.*

Minutes later, Clancy is out on the curb. He is putting the last of his tools into the bed of his pickup when Chloe Anderson backs her pearl white Lexus down the drive and onto the street. He makes his way around the bed of his truck and alongside the Lexus. Clancy recalls her scent, thinking of the panties balled up in his pants. Before pulling away, the wife turns to him. When she smiles and gives a slight wave, something twitches in Clancy's groin.

"See you soon, baby," he says, watching the Lexus disappear around a corner. "I'll see you real soon."

———

According to its Zen-inspired website, Ten Thousand Leaves is a resort and spa nestled among sixty sprawling acres of Maine's maples and birches. Modeled after the traditional Japanese mountain hot spring resorts, the handful of private cottages are all named for types of moons: New Moon, Rising Moon, Crescent Moon and so on. Each one has its own wood-burning fireplace, furnished robes called *yukatas*, a private meditative court-yard, bamboo mats and a personal servant called a *nakai*. All furnishings are specifically designed to promote a relaxing atmosphere with a focus on serenity and tranquility. In addition to the twelve miles of well-manicured and tree-lined walking paths, no less than three hot spring-fed *Rotenburo*, or open-air baths dot the property.

It certainly isn't the kind of place he would normally visit, whether he had the money or not. And he doesn't.

"Damn."

Clancy closes the lid to his laptop. He slides it onto the dashboard alongside the flower-shaped Post-It he slipped into his pocket when the husband wasn't looking. To each his own, but Clancy has no interest in spring-fed baths or meditative courtyards.

He is there for one thing and one thing only.

The Lexus sits in the front row of the parking lot. Clancy is parked in the rear and has yet to see the wife herself. It takes nearly two hours scrunched down in the cab of his truck before he catches a glimpse of her. A mulched walkway leads around the main building, then branches off in several directions toward cottages tucked into the woods. Any one of them could have led to hers. Luckily, Clancy spots her leaving the main building after what appears to have been a yoga session based on her attire. He sighs in relief. Going door to door would have drawn entirely too much attention.

When he exits the truck and follows her, Clancy is mindful to keep his distance. This isn't the first of what he likes to call his "surprise dates." He's thankful to learn that

that hers is the cottage located the farthest from the others. No less than fifty yards of sprawling oaks separate it from the nearest cottage. He smiles at how much privacy they'll enjoy. And, if things don't go smoothly, well then, that privacy will come even more in handy. He doesn't anticipate resistance on the wife's part. After all, she practically invited him. Why else would she have left the Post-It notepad where he could sneak it? But one never knows. His surprise dates haven't always gone smoothly.

Clancy raps his knuckles on the cottage's heavy wooden door and takes a deep breath. *Here we go.* He runs a hand through his hair, smoothing down the cowlick that creates a natural peak in the back. His mouth feels as if he has been eating sawdust. Moistening his lips, he waits patiently. After all, he has waited ten days already.

The chorus from Marvin Gaye's "Let's Get It On" is running through his head when the door opens.

"Hey, baby!" The wife's eyes, so bright and full of excitement one second, turn dark and quizzical. Seeing Clancy standing on the stoop, her brow wrinkles. She casts a glance past him before turning back. "Wha—what are you doing here? And how did you find me?"

Clancy's smile stretches from one side of his face to the other. His chest aches from the pounding of his heart. "Surprised?"

But the wife is either too caught off guard to speak or simply can't find the words. A wide-eyed stare is her only response. Within seconds, alarm registers on her face. She takes a step back from the doorway.

And then it hits Clancy like a bullet between the eyes: not only is she not expecting him, she is disturbed by his presence.

His smile fades.

"Again," she says, "what the hell are you—"

Clancy doesn't let her finish. With a hand to her sternum, he shoves the wife backward and follows her across the threshold of the tiny, one room cottage. He closes the door behind him with his foot.

His smile returns as he reaches up and slides his hand behind the wife's neck. Grasping a handful of silky blonde hair, Clancy pulls her head toward him. She starts to protest. He kisses her open mouth.

The wife places her hands against Clancy's chest, creating a barrier between them. "Stop it," she says, turning her head away. "Stop it now! What are you doing?" She uses the back of her hand to wipe Clancy's saliva from her lips.

Clancy is both disappointed and offended and hides neither fact. He drives all the way here and this is the reception he gets? Clancy shakes his head. He can't believe her lack of hospitality. He didn't expect it. Not from her. Especially since he'd been invited.

"So that little song and dance routine in your kitchen wasn't so I'd follow you?" The question is meant to be hypothetical. Clancy takes a step forward. "Bullshit. You wanted me to come. You've been throwing yourself at me since the first day I walked into your house. All but handed me that Post-It with the address of this place."

Clancy takes another step toward her.

The wife counters with a step back. "You need to leave right now. Or I fuckin' swear I'll call the police."

When the wife turns to grab her cell phone off the small table beside the bed, it only confirms Clancy's growing suspicions. He has been played all along. When she turns it on and starts tapping the screen, blood flushes Clancy's face. His jaw sets. Perspiration breaks out all over his body.

Clancy rushes forward. He tackles the woman onto the

bed, which is little more than a futon cushion thrown onto the bamboo floor. Her cell phone crashes to the floor. He's prepared for the barrage of flailing arms and fights them off as they come. He forces her face into a pillow and swings a leg over her back, pinning her down. A heel comes within inches of rendering his visit useless. It catches him mid-thigh instead. With a handful of hair, Clancy wrenches the woman's head back, straining the muscles in her throat. It is a time-honored move and renders the wife unable to scream.

A knock on the door brings everything to a halt. Clancy's attack ends abruptly, as does the wife's struggle against it. Both of them freeze, unsure what to do next.

Silence fills the room.

Maintaining pressure on the back of the wife's head, Clancy leans in and places his lips to her ear. "Expecting someone?" He keeps his voice low. "I was sure we'd be alone."

The wife still hasn't answered when a second knock rings out. Clancy entices her with another tug of her hair.

"It's probably the *nakai*." Her voice trembles as she keeps it just as low.

"The what?"

"The *nakai*. She's like a masseuse."

"Why would she be knocking on your door?" Clancy eases the pressure on the wife's head just slightly.

"I have a massage scheduled," the wife whispers through tears. "Here in the room."

Clancy bites his lip. He didn't plan on being interrupted. Wasn't escaping the world and getting away from it all the point of places like this? Clancy takes a moment to think. He hopes the woman at the door will go away while he does.

A third knock reverberates through the cottage, forcing

Clancy's hand. He releases the wife's hair and crawls off both her and the bed. He pulls his utility knife from its nylon pouch on his belt. He had hoped he wouldn't need it, but then nothing so far was going as planned. He slides the knife open.

"Move." Clancy flashes the blade so the woman can see what his mode of encouragement will be. When she is on her feet, he grabs her by the arm. "You don't feel well," he whispers, his lips against her ear. "You're sorry, but you need to cancel your appointment."

The woman wipes away tears. "And if she doesn't buy it?"

Clancy shakes the wife violently, then returns his lips to her ear. "Why wouldn't she?" To show that he doesn't expect an answer, he presses the handle of the utility knife into the small of her back.

Clancy maintains a constant grip on the wife's elbow as he walks her to the door.

"Okay," he says when the doorknob is within reach. But his thoughts are interrupted. A fourth, even more insistent knock rattles the door. "What the fuck?" Clancy shakes his head, purses his lips. "Fuckin' persistent, ain't she?"

Clancy turns the wife so that she's facing him. His eyes bore into hers, emphasizing what he's about to say. "Now, open the door, and make sure you do just as I said. She gives you any hassle, threaten to speak to her supervisor."

Turning loose the wife's arm, Clancy positions himself behind the door.

With the doorknob in hand, the wife glances once more at Clancy. Fear and tears fill her pleading eyes.

Clancy directs her with a nod.

After a soft click of the latch, the heavy, wooden door opens partway.

"Hello."

There's no reply to the wife's greeting. Even as the door stands open, nobody speaks. Neither the wife, nor the *nakai*. But there's something. An exchange. It is subtle, but Clancy catches an immediate twitch of the wife's head. Clancy wedges his face against the crack in the door, but it's too narrow to see who is standing on the stoop.

"I'm sorry," the wife says flatly. "I'm not feeling well." Her head twitches a second time.

Clancy feels his face flush. She's sending a signal! Waving them off. Alerting whoever is on the other side of the door. He drags the knife's blade across the grain of the door. The scratching sound is barely audible, but an effective reminder of the stakes.

"I'm sorry," the wife repeats, then closes the door.

Clancy immediately yanks the wife's arm, spinning her until they are face to face. "The hell was that?"

The wife stammers. Fear rims her wide eyes red. Whether it is fear of being discovered or of her overall predicament, Clancy can't be sure.

He gets up in the wife's face. "What the hell you tryin' to do?" Spittle hits her cheek as he speaks. "Something wrong with your head?"

The wife's jaw drops. "No! I swear!" Her hands go to Clancy's chest. "Please. Just relax. I promise I'm cooperating."

The wife runs her fingers between the buttons of Clancy's work shirt. They tickle the hairs. He acknowledges it for what it is: a good move on her part. She is trying to keep him calm, and Clancy can appreciate that. After all, her cooperation and returned affection is all he wants.

The wife's eyes flash to the window behind Clancy.

He hardly notices.

The wife's soothing hands continue to caress his chest.

His eyes drift closed. He breathes easier. His mouth is suddenly dry. Clancy fights to keep the ice in his veins from completely melting.

"I'm sorry." The wife's voice is low and breathy. Her words, seductive. "You caught me off guard, is all." She releases one of the buttons and slips her entire hand inside the front of his shirt. "We can do this. I mean, how rude am I? You came all this way just for me."

Clancy's mouth is like a barren and cracked desert. He licks his lips, but it helps little. Opening his eyes, he slides the blade back into the utility knife and tosses it onto the bed.

"That's more like it." He reaches up, glides his hands through the wife's blond hair and up her long neck. He takes her head in his hands. He leans in. She smells like rosewater, the same scent that permeates her bedroom at the house. He whispers in her ear, "We're gonna have so much—."

The pain in his groin is sudden and blinding. Clancy's breath catches in his throat. Doubling over, his hands release the wife and go immediately to his privates. He gasps for air that won't come. A sharp pain shoots through both kneecaps as they hit the floor.

The wife bolts for the door.

Clancy releases himself, reaches up in time to grab a back pocket of her white jeans. The fabric starts to rip, but enough of it holds, slowing her escape. Clancy pulls her back and away from the door.

"Bitch!"

The door to the cottage swings open, smashing into Clancy's hip. He howls in pain. A realization: *she didn't lock the door after closing it.*

A large man, a full foot taller than Clancy, rushes through the doorway. Fury sets his eyes ablaze. A growl, as animalistic as any Clancy has ever heard, erupts from the man's chest. A large hand immediately closes around Clancy's throat, lifting him off his knees.

He has no choice but to release the wife again.

She stumbles away.

A white flash blinds him. A stabbing pain shoots through Clancy's nose and up into his eyes. The man's fist connects a second time, returning Clancy to the floor. This time onto his back. He is not sure how long he holds on before his world shuts down and everything goes black.

———

Clancy awakens to a foggy mind and restraints binding his hands behind him. The taste of copper coats his mouth. His broken nose a reminder of what happened, because pain has a way of doing that. He is seated in a chair, presumably the one from the tiny desk against one of the walls. "For moments of reflection" the website had suggested. His legs won't move either. Thankfully, his eyes work, though the sight he sees upon opening them isn't a welcome one.

A pale, muscular rear pumps up and down on the bed. Beneath it lays the wife, her long, slender legs wrapped around the man's waist. Moans of passion, both male and female, fill the room.

Clancy's stomach turns. Bile rises.

A sudden cough betrays him and all activity on the bed comes to a halt.

The man raises his head in Clancy's direction. It is not the head of Mr. Anderson, and somehow Clancy knew it wouldn't be. A broad smile takes over the man's face.

Clancy's head is clearing, but his heart sinks. Something about the man's smile promises bad things for Clancy.

The man climbs off the bed. When he turns toward Clancy, his arousal points accusingly in Clancy's direction. Clancy tries to ignore it, but he can't tear his eyes from the opposing man in front of him. He is ripped from head to toe. His long black hair is slicked back, his chest a chiseled masterpiece. He stands well over six feet, and there is not one muscle in the man's form that hasn't benefitted from time in a gym.

Clancy is both impressed and humbled.

He draws his eyes away in time to catch a glimpse of the wife's bare chest before she grabs the sheet and parachutes it over her. Together, the man and wife form a scenario as absurd and infuriating as any Clancy can imagine. There is only one bright side: he's not the only one being played.

"Boyfriend, I assume?" Clancy's first attempt at speaking shoots a bolt of white hot pain through the right side of his face.

"Glad to see you're awake," the man says, stepping toward Clancy. Up close, the smile reveals perfect white teeth. "To be honest, fella, I wasn't expecting a threesome this weekend. But, hell, we can still have some fun." There is a wildness in the man's eyes. It speaks to the rage that comes from too many steroids. "But I gotta be honest. It may not be all that much fun for you."

Across the room, the wife rises from the bed. She wraps the rest of the sheet around her and glides like a ghost across the floor. Taking up a spot behind the boyfriend, she peers over her shoulder.

"What are you gonna do to him?" Her voice is languid. Her eyes look as though they have not only seen things, but fear seeing them again.

Clancy swallows hard.

"What are *we* gonna do with him, you mean."

The wife shrinks further behind the boyfriend. His arousal hasn't diminished, and if anything, it has grown by a measure. This disturbs Clancy in more ways than one. He struggles against the restraints on his wrists. The bindings feel flat and leathery. There is no give. Clancy envisions a belt doing the job. Dread falls over him.

"Like I said, *we* are gonna have some fun."

The boyfriend's fist comes out of nowhere. It catches Clancy on the left cheek. The chair rocks back on its hind legs, then settles forward. The pain in the left side of his face now mirrors that in his right. A fresh wave of coppery blood floods his mouth.

Clancy spits a mass of red phlegm at the boyfriend's feet.

Laughing, the boyfriend turns away, leaving the wife to stand awkwardly before Clancy. She doesn't make eye contact, but looks at the floor instead.

The boyfriend grabs a pair of jeans from the edge of the bed and slips them on. After buttoning them, he reaches for a belt that isn't there. "Oh, that's right." He grins at Clancy. "You're borrowing it at the moment." The laughter that follows is both sinister and mocking.

The temperature of Clancy's blood starts to drop.

Shaking her head, the wife escapes into the bathroom and closes the door behind her.

Barefoot and shirtless, the boyfriend makes his way over to the small table beside the bed.

The sound of metal scraping against glass echoes through the room. When the boyfriend turns around, he holds Clancy's utility knife in his hand. With a flip of his thumb, the shiny blade slides out of the end.

Clancy cringes and a shiver runs through him. His

heart starts to pound. The evening's festivities are about to begin. His mind splits in a million directions. None of them worthwhile. None of them good.

The boyfriend smiles. "So nice of you to bring a party favor." He strolls over to Clancy, turning the blade this way and that like he's imagining all of its varied uses. He kneels beside Clancy.

The blade is cold against his skin. When it moves, it traces a line down Clancy's neck and across his throat. But it doesn't cut him. At least he doesn't think so. There is no pain, no trickle of blood. The man is toying with him, trying to scare him, and Clancy hopes that's as far as things go.

If fear is the man's plan, he has already achieved his objective. A warm sensation dribbles down Clancy's leg. Sweat coats his body. He wants to swallow, but with the blade still to his throat, he fears a geyser of blood will be the result.

A knock at the cottage door keeps him from finding out.

Clancy's pounding heart leaps into his throat.

The boyfriend's smile fades. He turns and stares expectantly at the bathroom door. When the wife still hasn't emerged by the time a second knock comes, he rises. Tossing the utility knife onto the bed, the boyfriend crosses the room to the door. With his hand on the knob, he looks to Clancy.

"You open that mouth, I'll make sure it never opens again."

He doesn't wait for Clancy to respond. Instead, he swings the door wide. For several seconds, the boyfriend just stands there. He doesn't say anything, nor does he move. He is a wax statue.

From where Clancy sits, he can't see the boyfriend's

face. He has no clue what is going on, but envisions a tiny Japanese woman standing on the stoop gaping up at the giant of a man answering the door.

Out of nowhere, a strange thought hits Clancy. He wonders if the wife is allowed to have guests in the cottage. He certainly wouldn't mind being tossed out on his ear.

After a lifetime of anticipation, the boyfriend slowly backs away from the open door.

A raised pistol, its barrel a shiny nickel plate, follows the boyfriend into the room. At the end of the arm wielding the gun is a familiar face, albeit unwelcomed. Any hope of being saved by an immigrant masseuse slips away.

"Sit." The husband gestures toward the bed, kicking the door closed behind him. It's only then that he realizes he's not alone with the boyfriend. The husband's eyes double in size at the sight of Clancy. His mouth gapes. "The fuck?"

The husband's reaction tells Clancy that he'd expected one of them to be here, but not the other.

The husband's surprise is short-lived as the boyfriend takes a step toward him. The husband swings the gun back around, jamming the end of the barrel into the boyfriend's forehead. "I said sit, asshole!"

This time, the boyfriend complies, but not without a smirk. He shakes his head. "Like you're really gonna shoot me. I'm just screwin' her, dude. Not tryin' to steal her away or nothin'."

The husband's face blazes a deep red.

Clancy struggles to get his hands free, unsure how far the situation will escalate. He uses his fingers to try and find the belt buckle. When they find metal, his spirits raise. But, a sound from across the room stops his progress.

The wife emerges from the bathroom. A thick white robe has replaced the sheet. Her long blond hair is now pulled up into a bun that sits on top of her head. She gasps, calculating the scene she's just walked into. Her earlier looks of concern are replaced with horror. She stands frozen.

For several tense moments, nobody moves, nobody speaks. Clancy's eyes pinball around the room, darting from one person to another, wondering who's going to make the first move. Sweat runs down his temple. His heart wants to explode through his chest. He can only imagine where things will go from here. And for the first time since he met the wife, he wishes he hadn't.

The husband is the first to speak. The barrel of the gun accentuates the trembling of his hand. "Ya know, I had my suspicions, but I hoped like hell I was wrong."

"Baby—"

"Shut up!" The gun swings away from the boyfriend and takes dead aim at the wife. The end of the barrel trembles more than ever. "You don't get to speak, and you sure as hell don't get to call me baby. Not anymore."

The boyfriend laughs. "Damn, fella. A bit dramatic, aren't we?"

Clancy swallows hard.

The husband keeps the gun trained on his wife, but his eyes turn their fury on the boyfriend. Someone is at the end of his rope. His lips are pursed, his jaw is locked hard. Perspiration glistens on the husband's forehead.

Thankful to be the least of everyone's worries, Clancy takes advantage of their focus being elsewhere. While his eyes keep watch on the room, he once again struggles against the restraints binding his wrists. His fingertips walk the length of the belt and find the end. The discovery propels him straighter in the chair. Reason for hope. He maintains a poker face as he begins to work the length of belt backward through the buckle.

"What the hell do you know?" Spittle flies from the husband's mouth. His eyes are glassy and rimmed with redness. "You obviously have no respect for marriage."

"Matthew—"

The husband takes his eyes off the boyfriend to glare at the wife. He opens his mouth to speak…

The boyfriend makes a move.

The gun swings around and barks loudly.

The boyfriend's head snaps backward. The back of it explodes in a blossom of red mist, ruining the white sheets and pillows. When the boyfriend's head recoils, there's a small, perfectly round hole above his left eye. It starts to leak as his body begins a slow retreat sideways onto the bed. A confused expression spreads across his face.

The wife screams. Her hands spring up to cover her eyes.

Clancy's jaw drops. His fingers fall idle, momentarily forgetting the restraints. Absolute fear overcomes him.

Hysterical screaming fills the tiny room as the wife pushes her throat to its limits.

The husband turns the gun on his wife.

"Shut up!"

But she doesn't. She screams like she can't help herself; like she knows no other reaction.

"Chloe, dammit! Shut it!" The trembling in the husband's hand becomes uncontrollable. He lowers the shaking gun and steps toward his wife.

Clancy is mesmerized. He tries to anticipate what will happen next, but can't even fathom. He only knows that he must get out. Some way, somehow. His fingers come alive. Clancy finds the pin securing the belt to the buckle and works it through the hole in the leather.

The wife stops screaming long enough to call the husband a bastard. Her eyes are red and draining themselves of tears. She rushes the husband and starts pounding his chest with balled up fists. Each blow elicits a hollow thud.

For a time, the husband withstands the abuse. He offers no other recourse than to turn his face away. It's only when the wife rears back and spits into his face that he reacts. Still gripping the gun in one, the husband lays his hands against the wife's shoulders and gives her a hard shove.

Clancy jumps at the crack of another gunshot. The chair rocks sideways, but remains upright.

A look of shock comes over the wife's face. A hole behind her ear starts to expel blood. When the bullet exited the other side of her head, it shattered a glass bowl perched on a shelf behind her. Glass, black stones, and bamboo crash to the floor a second before the wife's crumpled body.

Shock grips Clancy, paralyzing him. There is nothing left to hope for. Death is a certainty.

A pool of blood spreads across the floor.

The husband's wide eyes and gaping mouth suggest an accident. The wail of anguish as he falls to his knees beside his wife confirms it. When the husband takes her lifeless body in his arms, her head lolls to one side. Her arms fall limp. Blood streams from the massive wound, staining her white robe. Cries of the wife's name are mixed with sobs and mutterings of apology.

Clancy has the belt through the buckle and the pin out of the hole when the husband gently lays the wife onto the floor. Shaking with terror, Clancy stops fumbling. When the husband picks up the gun, Clancy stops breathing. He prepares to beg for his life.

The husband turns the gun on himself, nesting it against his temple.

Clancy starts to call out, but is unsure why. It doesn't matter. The words won't come.

A third squeeze of the trigger silences the husband's sobs. He falls backward, blank eyes rolling toward the ceiling. The gun drops from his hand and skids across the highly-polished bamboo floor.

Clancy releases the breath he's been holding. He gulps air, forcing it into his lungs. He wonders if this is what it means to hyperventilate.

A nauseating stench fills the room. Blood and gunpowder create a sickening combination. Bile churns in Clancy's stomach as the pool of blood from the husband spreads across the floor and joins the pool from the wife. Drawn only minutes apart, two distinct shades of oxygenated red are already discernable.

With the pin free of the hole, Clancy slides the leather strap free from the buckle. He wrestles his hands out of the loops and the belt clatters to the floor. His wrists are chafed, and he starts to rub the pain away. His hands have turned a light purple. He shakes them to get the blood flowing. His skin quickly returns to its natural color.

A knock on the door.

Clancy freezes. *Who the fuck?* Then he remembers the gunshots. As far away from the other cottages as they were, it's very possible the shots were heard by someone. Clancy looks upon the room and the bloodbath it has become. Being the only person alive in a room full of murder means that one threat still remains: the threat of taking the fall.

Clancy works feverishly on the bindings that still restrain his ankles. Thankfully, they prove easier to escape. Once untied, he finds the restraints were simple t-shirts, twisted into thick ropes. He drops them to the floor and stands.

His legs are shaky.

His head swims.

The doorknob turns.

Clancy shuffles over and positions himself behind the door, but not before collecting the belt. He wraps each end around a hand, pulling it tight between them. As he waits, his eyes fall on the chair and the t-shirts laying beneath it. Does it look like a fourth person was in the room? It does, and it doesn't. But Clancy can't worry about it now.

The door creaks as it opens.

"Mrs. Anderson?" The voice is soft and accented. *The nakai.* "You've missed your appointment. Mrs. Anderson?"

Clancy raises the belt chest high. The muscles in his forearms burn with rigidity. He is poised to strike just as soon as the *nakai* shows herself. He is not taking the fall for what happened in the room. Not a chance. He takes a deep breath, holds it.

A small-framed, Japanese woman in a white *komono* shuffles into the cottage. Her steps are slow, unsure, as she calls the wife's name once more.

Clancy's chest aches with anticipation. He raises the belt. His hands shake.

The tiny woman draws in a sharp breath. She rushes past the doorway, past Clancy, and makes her way to the wife. The *nakai* kneels on the floor beside the fallen wife, her back to Clancy.

He stands dumbstruck, unsure what to do. He takes a silent step in her direction, belt raised. A sound from outside the cottage catches Clancy's attention. The rustling of leaves. He turns toward the sound and realizes there may be another way.

The front door stands wide open.

Opportunity.

Slowly and as quietly as possible, Clancy steps around the wooden door and out into the night. The world outside the cottage is darker than when he entered. With the belt still wrapped around his hands, Clancy weaves his way up the path toward the parking lot. The soft mulch silences his hurried steps. He is thankful for the cover of night. He dares not look behind him.

Opening the truck door, Clancy tosses the belt onto the passenger seat. Only once he has climbed in and closed the door behind him does he allow himself to breathe. The ache in his chest is crippling. He slouches in the seat. He lays his head back. He closes his eyes. Doing so brings up images from inside the cottage: the bodies, the blood, the way the wife's robe fell open when she went to the floor.

He can't help but smile. It was still one hell of a chest.

Clancy feels both sick to his stomach and excited at the same time. He realizes that, despite everything he has just witnessed, his desire is not deterred. He knows it should be and wonders what that says about him.

The sound of distant sirens force Clancy's eyes open. He sits up straight. With the sound growing louder, he turns on the ignition and puts the truck in gear.

At the entrance to the parking lot, Clancy can see the flashing blue lights that accompany the sirens. They are coming from the east and still at least a mile away. He relaxes a bit. Taking a right out of the resort's parking lot, he heads west.

His thoughts turn to other opportunities. As the truck rambles down the darkened road, Clancy thinks about a young single-mother who lives only a few miles away. Her newly remodeled bathroom had taken him only five days to complete. She had been so appreciative, and even admitted to being a little sad he'd finished the job so soon. She'd been thankful for his company.

Clancy looks at the clock on the dash, then over at the belt sitting on the seat beside him. The night is still young, and he can't wait to see the look on the mother's face when he shows up for their surprise date.

———

The two most common questions I get asked about my writing are "where do you get your ideas?" and "is there any money in it?" While the answer to the second question is a resounding "hell no," to the first question, my answer is usually "anywhere and everywhere." Sometimes story ideas come while I'm commuting to and from work. (I log many hours behind a steering wheel each week.) Other ideas come while I'm lying in bed almost asleep, and I have to jump up and jot them down lest I forget them by morning. (I've tried remembering without writing them down. It doesn't work.)

Then there are times I will be sitting in a barber's chair getting my hair cut and overhear a conversation that sparks an idea for a story. For "No Saints Here," that was exactly the case. I was getting my hair cut and overheard my stylist talking about a family member buying her a weekend at a spa. At the time, I thought it was a really nice and thoughtful gesture. But on my nearly forty-minute commute home that afternoon, somehow my mind was able to take that really thoughtful gesture and twist it into something much more demented. What ifs started flying like bullets and many had the same effect. When it was all said and done and the smoke had cleared, I had a storyline for one of the more brutal stories I've ever written. (And one of the most liked, so I'm not sure what that says about the people I associate with.)

So, thanks, Amanda, for planting the seed. I'm just glad your weekend turned out better than these poor people's.

Pigs

The farm was like any I had seen on television or the movies. A white, two-story house sat at the end of a long, dusty driveway. Modest, clapboard, full of Midwestern charm. A barn, which I suspected leaned a little more than when it was first built, loomed off to one side. Wood fencing sectioned off a portion of the property beside the barn. I assumed a livestock pen of some sort. And surrounding it all were rows of corn stalks that spread as far as the eye could see in any direction.

Having grown up in the trendy North Side neighborhood of Pittsburgh, I couldn't have been more out of my element if I'd found myself at the bottom of the ocean.

As I pulled up the dusty drive, an older gentleman dressed head to toe in denim stood with arms crossed and one foot on a lower fence rail. His boots and pant legs were caked with dried mud. His ball cap, a green mesh, faded by years of work in the sun. He watched long enough for me to shut off the engine and open my car door before turning away. I would soon find that offering me his backside would be the extent of his greeting. Not that I was expecting much of a reception. I was, after all, uninvited.

Grabbing my camera case off the passenger seat, I shut the car door and made my way over to the wooden pen.

According to the calendar, September was about to surrender to October. But at five o'clock that afternoon, the temperature was still pushing ninety. Sweat beaded on my forehead. I wiped it off with my hand, then wiped my hand on my cargo pants. I stopped a few feet short of the enclosure. Preferring to live a relatively solitary life through the lens of a camera, meeting new people presented an unsavory detour from that existence. This time proved no different. Walking up to the farmer, I felt like one of those guys in white shirts and black pants that ride their bicycles around, knocking on doors and handing out pamphlets. The guys people complain about.

"Good afternoon!"

The farmer simply looked me up and down, then turned back to what appeared to be a half-dozen pigs. No smile. No words of salutation. Just a nod. I took in a deep breath, slowly let it out and closed the gap between us.

The closer I got to the pen, the more the pigs came into view. They were massive. To say that even the smallest outweighed me by three or four times would be an understatement. And by the looks of the mess in the pen, they ate and shit more than I did, too. Surprisingly, doing both in the same place didn't seem to bother them. And here I had always heard how smart pigs were.

"Was wondering if you might be the owner of the cabin on the other side of that corn field."

The farmer looked toward the treetops that loomed in the distance beyond the rows of corn. He cleared his throat, then spat something dark and wet into the pen. "Be mine alright."

The pigs converged on the tobacco-colored phlegm with a voraciousness that caused a sick feeling to wash through my stomach. The largest of the six, a filthy, spotted son of a bitch the size of a small car, shoved his way to the front. But he was too late. The treat was gone. With a swiftness I wouldn't have expected, the large pig turned and chomped down on the ear of the one nearest by. The assaulted squealed and pulled away, leaving a small sliver of its ear between the larger pig's teeth.

"Um, cool." I hoped the farmer knew I was referring to the fact that he owned the cabin, not the act of swine cannibalism I'd just witnessed. I tried not to look too disgusted. I doubted I did a very good job. Natural selection had an entirely different meaning in the city. "Well, sir, I was wondering if you might be willing to rent the cabin to me for a couple nights. I'm a photographer and looking to hole up in the area. Get some nature shots. That cabin would be a perfect home base."

As I spoke, the farmer's focus remained on his quarrelsome pigs. Lost in thought as he was, he took forever to answer. When the old man finally tore his eyes off the animals and met mine, a wry smile cracked his otherwise stoic face. "Why sure." He lifted his ball cap and wiped his brow with a tightly buttoned sleeve. "That'd be just fine."

"Cool," I said, before I could stop myself. I really needed another phrase. I was coming off like a broken record. An illiterate one at that.

"Have to leave your car here, though." The farmer once again spat into the pen. The pigs once again scrambled after the treat. This time, the largest of the six got his way, but that didn't stop the others from going after it. Apparently, pigs have short term memories. "Ain't no driveway to the cabin, only a narrow path through the field. I'd let you use my four-wheeler, but she's got a busted tranny."

I shook my head, relieved at how easily I was granted permission. "That's not a problem." I had seen a gravel pull-off just down the road from the cabin. It was probably closer. But leaving my car on the side of a rarely-traveled road in the middle of nowhere probably wasn't a good idea. I gestured toward my car. "Is it in the way right there?"

The farmer brought his foot down off the rail. It was only then that I noticed his body hunched to one side as he stood. I assumed he had back problems or issues with his hip. He was, after all, an older gentleman, and it's not like farming was easy work. In looking over my car, the old man lost himself in contemplation. Silence drug on for several seconds. I was about to speak up when he finally said, "Should be fine. Need it moved, I'll come find ya."

I stopped myself from using the word "cool" again and simply nodded.

It didn't take long to find that the farmer's hospitality only reached so far. It wasn't that I was ungrateful, but we must have looked odd as we walked the path through the cornfield. While his arms swung empty at his sides, mine were loaded down with my duffle bag, two camera cases and a large cooler full of mostly beer and bottled water that I dragged along the ground behind me. But he was old and walked with a hitch, so I guess that was excuse enough for not lending me a hand.

I tried not to judge.

The path was mostly dirt and parted the field like the Red Sea. Rolling oceans of corn spread for miles on either side. The six-foot tall stalks swayed to and fro thanks to a breeze that my five-foot-eight frame couldn't feel, yet longed to in the afternoon heat. Beads of sweat trickled down my temple. My tee shirt clung to my damp skin.

"So, you take pictures?" The farmer spat on the ground in front of us, forcing me to sidestep the brown wad. He did nothing of the sort and squished the tiny puddle of phlegm with the edge of his boot.

"Yes, sir." I stopped for a moment and wiped my sweaty hand on my pants before picking up the cooler. Once I'd fallen back in step with the man, the conversation continued.

"And whatcha do with these pictures after ya take 'em?"

"Sell a few. Magazines. Websites mostly." We navigated around a rather deep trench cutting through the path. A person could easily snap an ankle. I would have to remember it if I ever found myself out there at night. "Sometimes I'll enter one in a contest. But generally, I end up keeping most for myself."

The farmer stopped and turned to me. "There much money in that? Taking pictures and keepin' 'em for yourself?" His eyebrow cocked downward. It hinted at more than a little mockery in his query.

"No," I said. "Not generally." I looked up the path that seemingly went on forever. I couldn't yet see the cabin and wondered how much further we needed to go. "That's why I don't stay at the Hilton when I travel, either."

I chuckled, but my humor was lost on the old man. Not even a smile. With a simple shrug of his shoulders, he turned and continued along the path, while I made a mental note to save my wit for those who would appreciate it.

After several more laborious minutes, a rusted metal roof finally rose above the corn tassels. A few steps more and the rest of the cabin came into view. With a porch that wouldn't stop a ball from rolling, and weeds that grew wherever they damn well felt like, the structure looked about as luxurious from the front as it had from behind.

"So, if you don't mind me asking, why'd you put a cabin all the way back here?" I hitched my slipping duffle bag further up my shoulder. "Seems like an odd location."

The farmer didn't miss a beat. "Good place for shootin' things." Then he chuckled. "And I ain't talkin' about your kinda shootin'." He pointed a finger pistol at me and pulled the trigger. "We don't use no cameras."

My pace slowed. "I'm sorry?"

"Deer. Pheasant. A coyote or two," said the farmer over his shoulder. "Was a huntin' cabin at one time. Been sittin' empty for a while now. Ever since…the accident."

But instead of explaining further, the old man just kept on walking. I considered asking what accident had brought about a stop to his use of the cabin, but decided to leave well enough alone. It truly didn't concern me, and the more I thought about it, I didn't much care anyway. I was just eager to get to the cabin and away from the strange old man.

Where the cornfield ended, the dirt path gave way to grass. What would be considered the front yard looked to have been left to its own devices. Tall, thick and out of control, it was obvious that the grass hadn't been mowed in some time. Neither had the weeds.

Sadly, the abandonment wasn't restricted to the yard. The cabin's wood siding had weathered to a light grey. Dark green algae crept down from the eaves. The covered, yet sloping porch stretched across the entire front. A couple of windows peeked out from beneath the roof's overhang, but otherwise, the front of the cabin was pretty much a blank slate. No handcrafted ironwork decorated the front, no whimsical strands of chili pepper party lights draped from one corner to the other. The rustic cabin provided shelter, simple as that.

"Here we are."

As we took our first steps onto the porch, the wood creaked under our weight. The planks were as weathered as the siding and splitting. Ambitious dandelions grew up through the cracks. Based on the level of neglect I had seen to that point, I couldn't help but wonder what horrors awaited me on the inside. Images of a Halloween-type display of cobwebs came to mind.

I was surprised when the farmer went right for the doorknob and pushed open the door. A feeling of insecurity immediately followed.

"Sorry." The farmer shot me a knowing glance. "Ain't never had no need for a lock."

"That's fine," I said with a smile. It actually wasn't fine, but I was a beggar in a chooser's world. I made a mental note to put something in front of the door that night while I slept.

The creaking didn't stop once we set foot inside. And this time, I wasn't surprised. The scarred and somewhat warped floorboards appeared in only slightly better shape than the ones on the porch. The gaps between a few were even wide enough for a flattened hand to fit through. I tried not to imagine what awfulness might lay in the dark crawlspace beneath my feet. My mind conjured some possibilities anyway. The downside of having an overactive imagination.

Ultimately, it was the stench of the cabin that frightened me the most. I was expecting musty, but was hit with rot instead. My eyes watered. Nausea became a real thing. The farmer seemed not to notice.

On the growing list of things that the cabin needed, some fresh air topped the list.

I dropped the cooler beside a ratty, moth-eaten couch. I set the two camera cases on top of the cooler. Who knew what colonies of insect made their homes inside that old piece of furniture? I kept my duffle over my shoulder as I made my way to the nearest window.

Pulling open the curtains sent clouds of dust billowing into the air. The tiny particles hovered in the room, caught in the first rays of sunlight in who knew how long. A cough crept up, but I stifled it so as not to be rude. My throat burned for the effort.

The latches on the window were unlocked. I gave the wood sash a shove upward and hustled out of the pall of dust. Warm, clean air followed me into the room.

"You can join the missus and me for supper tonight if you're of mind. Best pork butt in the state. Taters, beans, all the fixin's. That is, if you don't already have a better standing offer."

I didn't. My camera, a couple cold beers and this cabin would be the extent of my social life for the next couple days. Besides, most of my meals anymore came by way of a bag, a box or wrapped in a napkin from one of the vendors in Pittsburgh's Food Truck Park. Despite the fact the lingering odor had stolen my appetite, a home cooked meal actually sounded nice. At some point.

"That'd be great," I said. "Thank you."

The farmer replied with a nod of his cap and nothing more. No smile or change in his expression of any kind. He could not have cared less whether I accepted or declined his offer. For him and his generation, it was simply customary to ask.

"I'll leave you to it, then."

"Wait!" I reached into my duffle, rooted around and pulled out my wallet. "What do I owe you?"

The farmer eyed the leather tri-fold in my hand. His

brow lifted. He bit his lip. After a moment's hesitation, he shook his head. "We'll settle up at dinner tonight." And with another nod, the farmer turned and exited the cabin, closing the door behind him.

I didn't like the sound of that. *We'll settle up at dinner tonight.* I envisioned myself washing the dishes or giving the old man and his wife candlelit foot massages. I would have rather just paid a little money.

I made my way around the rest of the one-room cabin. Opening the last two drapes sent out the same hack-worthy plumes of dust as the first. I shook my head. If I made it through the next couple days without developing a lung disease, it would be a miracle. As the cloud of dust settled onto the set of twin beds sitting side by side, I decided then and there I would be sleeping in my clothes. If I slept at all.

I was about to investigate where the rotten smell was coming from when it dawned on me: the farmer hadn't told me what time to be up for dinner.

I rushed to the door, hoping to still catch him within earshot. It had, after all, been a few minutes since he had left. The chances weren't good.

When I threw open the cabin door, I nearly ran into the old farmer. Framed by the doorway, his silhouette blocked out enough of the fading sun that his features were lost in shadow. I couldn't see his face, but his crooked posture was a dead giveaway.

"Oh, sorry." I took a step back, my surprise calling the shots. *Wait a second. Why was he still standing there? And why the hell was I apologizing?* A chill rattled my shoulders despite the afternoon heat. Something about the old man hovering there didn't feel right. It took me a second to regain my composure. Once I did, I tried my best to disguise my unease. "Hey, was just gonna ask—"

"Let's say seven." The farmer looked me up and down once more, but ignored the fly that seemed to have an unhealthy interest in his ear. After a few seconds, he turned away. Three steps later and he was off the porch.

This time, I stood at the door, watching as he crossed through the grass. Only once he had started up the path did I close the door.

"Weird," I said, turning back to the cabin. "So weird." The fact that the old man had remained on the porch for so long after supposedly leaving was a little unsettling. Had he been watching me through the window? And why had it seemed like he was still sizing me up before finally leaving?

I settled on the notion that the old man had, in fact, started up the path, but had turned back when he realized he hadn't given me a time. At least that was the explanation that didn't leave me all creeped out. I had others. They didn't bode well. I put them out of my mind.

Over the next few minutes, I busied myself trying to find out where that awful smell was coming from. It didn't take long. My first guess was the right one. The kitchen.

The odor grew stronger the closer I drew to the heart of the cabin. Stepping up to the sink was a PETA member's nightmare come true. A blood-crusted ten-inch carving knife teetered on the edge of an equally blood-crusted sink. Blood coated the countertop, the thin layer brown and flaky. Dried bits of flesh and muscle gathered near the drain, caught in the basket strainer. Coarse hair stuck to everything, and the entire scene had the look of age.

A grimy diagram on how to section off various animals hung by a piece of tape from an overhead cabinet.

My stomach roiled. Suddenly, the open windows weren't cutting it. I needed real fresh air. Even the tiny window above the sink wouldn't have helped. Not to mention it was hazed over and splattered with blood, so I wasn't going to touch it anyway.

I stepped out onto the porch where a warm breeze carried the rot away. I sucked in several deep breaths, all while thinking my choice in lodging needed a serious upgrade. Someone needed to sell some photographs. And soon.

Shadows from the nearby corn almost reached the porch. The sun was making its decent. I looked at the watch my father had gifted me for being accepted into Rutgers. A gift he had almost taken back when I told him I would be majoring in photography. *That's not a steady career. Do you wanna spend your life hungry or something?* If he'd said it once, he had said it a hundred times, doing his best to dissuade me. But I remained steadfast in my decision.

And I hated that he had been right.

According to the watch, it was going on six o'clock. Besides having to be up at the house for dinner around seven, I estimated I had less than an hour before the surrounding landscape turned black with night. Not the most desirable way to make my way through a corn field, designated path or not. I had seen entirely too many horror films that started with that exact premise.

Grabbing a bottle of water and shoving it in one of my cargo pockets, I ventured out into the yard, camera in hand.

The sound of crickets welcomed me. Despite the fact the sun was going down, the air remained thick with early autumn humidity. The sky blazed a campfire orange with ribbons of pink and purple coursing throughout. The moon, its crescent waning, was already making an appearance.

The hoo-hoo of an owl came from somewhere in the distance.

I wanted to stop here and there, get some shots of the corn at dusk. Maybe from near the ground. The tips of the stalks were turning a brittle brown, and the color contrast against the vivid sky would make for some great imagery.

I had no sooner crossed through the grass and onto the dirt path when I got the brilliant idea of getting some shots of the corn from within the corn looking out before it got too dark. I took a moment to check myself and determine if it was something I really wanted to attempt. Doing whatever it takes to get the best shot possible is what drives an artist, separates the professional from the hobbyist, all that stuff. Even so, I had to admit that entering a large cornfield at dusk was uncharacteristic of me. Not to mention, a tad foolish. A moment later, despite the nagging voice in my head urging against it, my artistic side won out.

With a deep breath and a dramatic farewell glance up and down the path, I slipped in between two rows of corn.

Growing up, the closest I ever came to being on a farm was when my parents dragged me to the local farmers market on the third Saturday of every month. I had never had occasion to wander through a cornfield before. Much less at dark. My excitement over the experience played out through the adrenalin pumping through me. Shadows of the towering stalks stretched into those of others from the next row. Together, they created a darkness deeper within their margins than out on the path. Inside the corn, night was already falling. Long, crinkled leaves brushed against my arms as the field swallowed me up. The only sky I could see was just above me. Fallen debris littered the ground below. I crunched my way through a minefield of dropped cobs and casted off husks. My hands parted curtains of stalks as I blazed my own path toward the farmhouse.

It didn't take long before I got the feeling I was being watched.

I didn't know who or from where, but the sensation of eyes on me was strong. I stopped, looked all around. All I saw were stalks of corn, their bounty pointed to the sky. I shrugged my shoulders and continued walking.

I had taken only a few steps before stopping again. Was I still going in the right direction? I didn't know, and the corn was too tall for me to see over. I had started in the direction that would lead me up to the farmhouse, but after zig-zagging through row after row the last five minutes, how could I be sure I was still on the right track?

My heart started to beat just a little faster.

Sweat ran down the side of my face.

Taking photos became a distant memory.

And while I stood in the middle of the field trying to figure out whether or not to turn back, the feeling of being watched never wavered.

"Hello?" I shouted. No answer.

I couldn't stay out there all night. I took a step in what I thought was the right direction. Rather, hoped. Then I took another. I stepped up my pace almost to a light jog, going down one row, then cutting over to the next when it felt necessary.

A dark figure loomed ahead. I stopped walking and crouched down, heavy breathing expanding and contracting my chest. A form created a void in the mass of stalks about twenty feet in front of me. Someone else was in the corn field. A worker? A farmhand I hadn't seen while up at the pen? Night was approaching fast, stealing the light and making it near impossible to discern whom it might be.

Part of me wanted to approach, hoping that whomever

it was would lead me out of the field. Part of me wanted to turn and run like hell.

I rose and started creeping toward the figure. Brittle corn husks crunched under foot. The closer I drew, the harder my heart pounded.

For their part, the figure didn't move, didn't make a sound. They just stood there. What would they be doing out there if not working?

Turns out, they *were* working. At least they were doing what they were supposed to. But it wasn't a person after all, and the discovery both relieved and disappointed me.

A cross had been fashioned by what appeared to be two long-handled broomsticks. A soiled, red flannel shirt draped over the cross, the horizontal broomstick acting as arms. The vertical broomstick was staked deep into the cracked earth.

And a rotted pig's head sat on top.

I gasped when I saw it.

The eye sockets were hollow, eyeballs gone. More than likely pecked out by the same birds it was fashioned to scare away. Its snout was wrinkled, the hide cracked and split. Two yellowed fangs, one on each side, protruded up from the closed mouth. One stuck straight up, the other pushed slightly outward, a mind of its own. Dried, leathery meat hung from the ragged wound where its neck had been severed. Blood had drained out, covering the top half of the shirt and broomstick. The red fluid had long ago baked to a midnight black by the sun.

The photographer in me that was intrigued by such a ghastly sight leaned in closer to get a better look.

"Boo!"

The raspy voice cut through the cacophony of crickets and sent me bolting upright. I reacted so harshly, I think my heart stopped beating. I know my hands jerked because

I dropped my camera. If my feet didn't leave the ground, it was only because they were momentarily frozen in place.

I managed to free them enough to spin around.

The old farmer stood behind me, his head poking through a wall of corn stalks. His laughter drowning out the crickets.

"What the hell, man?" Respect and courtesy went out the window, hand in hand. My stomach was in my throat. My heart was making a case for busting through my ribcage. "Seriously?"

The old man, on the other hand, acted as if this was the best laugh he'd had in years. "Should see your face." He was beside himself, slapping his knees and everything.

I bent down and picked up my camera. I dusted it off, but from the looks of it, it wasn't the worse for wear.

The old man's laughter died. "Hey, ah, sorry about that. Didn't know you'd scare so easy."

"It's okay," I lied. Turning the camera over in my hand, I said, "It

doesn't appear to be broken." We stood there for the minute it took me to verify that it wasn't. I draped the strap around my neck so I couldn't drop it again.

The old farmer removed his cap, smacked it across his thigh a couple times. Dust bloomed in the air. Pulling out a wrinkled red bandana, he wiped his face, starting with his forehead. Replacing his cap, the farmer looked at me with narrowed eyes, which did nothing to ease my still-firing nerves. He rubbed his hand over the three-day stubble on his chin. "Anyway, came lookin' for you. Heard you trompin' around in here."

Tromping? I hadn't been tromping any more than I had been dancing naked and singing show tunes.

"You'd be shit as a hunter, so's you know."

I shot a quick glance at my watch. I had to hold it at a

certain angle in order to read the face in the diminished light. "It's only a little after six."

"Yeah, well." The intensity of the farmer's demeanor sobered as he turned his eyes to the sky. A faint light emanated from the direction of what I assumed was his house. He seemed to focus on it. "Since you're here, thought maybe you could give me a hand with something before supper."

The old man must not ask for many favors, because he didn't seem comfortable with it. Still, it didn't stop him from asking. When he declined my offer to pay him for use of the cabin, it should have been my first clue that I would be doing some work at some point. I wondered if we were about to settle up.

My elevated heart rate reminded me that maybe I was the one who should be looking for compensation. "No problem," I muttered.

"Glad it's still workin'," said the farmer, pointing at my camera. "You'll wanna get a shot of this." Then he gestured for me to follow.

I took a step forward, then stopped. "By the way," I said, pointing at the pig's head, "that's just gross. You couldn't have used a pumpkin like everyone else?"

The farmer took an exaggerated look around. "You see any pumpkins since you pulled up? Pigs and corn, s'all I got."

I followed the farmer through the cornfield the best I could. The sun had officially set and night was upon us. Moonlight only marginally penetrated the dense field. The old man didn't seem to have a problem with any of it. He moved swiftly about the stalks of corn as if he were on a mission. Hitch in his gitty up and all. And since I was both impressed and completely unnerved by my surroundings, I wondered if the guy was planning on walking me back to the cabin after dinner, or if I would be on my own. Either way, I planned on the dirt path being under my feet.

"You know," the farmer said, parting his way through the corn, "pigs are a savage animal. A hog eats something, he eats it all. Even the bones. Chomp right through 'em like they're provin' a point. Makes an God awful, unnatural sound."

My stomach soured as I imagined such a sound. I could practically hear the snapping of bones being ground up in the pigs' powerful jaws. I shivered the sound away, though remnants of it remained.

I didn't ask the old man why he was telling me this, but the question was on my mind. His biology lesson served only to put my nerves even more on edge. A pig's ability to devour meat and bone certainly wasn't the type of small talk I would have chosen for our nighttime stroll through the cornfield. Nor did I have a clue as to what the old man was asking of me.

Tension gripped the back of my neck. The crickets continued to chatter. The breeze returned, swaying the tops of the cornstalks. And the faint glow rising from the farmhouse joined the moon as the only light around.

It was the perfect setting for a John Carpenter classic.

I tried to moisten my lips, but my mouth was bone dry.

Minutes later, the cornfield spit us out, depositing us onto the driveway some thirty yards from my car.

When the old man veered toward the pigpen, I reluctantly followed, casting a longing glance toward the house. It taunted me, so many of its interior lights on. The fact that we were heading in the opposite direction saddened me. After being tutored on the eating habits of pigs, the last thing I wanted was to saddle up close to one. Much less six.

"Teeth and hair," the farmer said, approaching the pen. He rested his arms across the top rail, the toe of his boot on the bottom. The half dozen filthy animals created a mini-stampede in his direction, each nudging and shoving the others out of their path. Not surprisingly, the largest among them positioned himself front and center. "'Bout the only parts their digestive systems can't process. Teeth and hair."

Sweat loitered on the back of my neck and forehead. I looked once more at my car. It now sat what felt like an insurmountable fifty feet away. I could make a break for it, I told myself. I could drive away and never look back, put the crazy farmer and his ravenous pigs behind me. That is, if I made it to the car.

Good place for shootin' things.

I stepped up to the railing.

I wiped away the sweat before it could drip into my eyes.

"Now, these here pigs," the farmer continued, "they ain't been fed for two days. They're hungry as all get out. Probably eat just about anything that finds its way in that there pen."

I instinctively raised my camera, wielding it like a weapon.

The old man looked at me and smiled weakly. "Which makes your arrival damn perfect timing."

I took a step back and not so subtly checked my pocket for car keys. I was of the mindset that my departure was long overdue. My welcome long overstayed.

That was about the time the farmer grabbed hold of the top rail and hoisted himself up. To my astonishment, the pigs instantly whipped themselves into a frenzy. One after another snapped at the farmer's boots, now planted dangerously within their reach. They nipped at each other.

Hungry grunts and excited squeals filled the night air. The docile pen was docile no longer.

One would have thought it was feeding time.

With a final look toward his house, the farmer swung one leg over the top rail, then the other.

At least, I think that's what happened.

The pigs were on him in the time it took me to blink. Grabbing ahold of his leg, the larger, heavier hog pulled the farmer off the railing and down into the mud. He landed with a splat. The other pigs converged on the old man like half-starved eating machines. The nauseating sound of gnashing teeth and grunts brought about the first scream.

My jaw dropped.

My mind exploded with fear.

I stood frozen, my brain grappling, and watched the escalating horror play out through the wooden slats of the railing.

The screams continued, each more ineffable than the previous. A sound like the ripping of heavy fabric erupted from the pile. A slick black substance began to wash over the pigs.

My stomach turned. Bile rose up, burning the back of my throat. I had never seen so much blood.

Just as quickly as they had started, the screams stopped. What replaced them wasn't any better, a sickening gurgling sound. A crunch here, a shred there. The farmer's face was gone.

My camera trembled in my hands. *Should I be shooting this?* Then another more disturbing thought hit me: is that what the old man had wanted? Was his intention for me to document his death for some strange reason?

You'll wanna get a shot of this.

One of the pigs buried its face in the farmer's crotch.

Another severed a leg just above the kneecap. The largest of the pigs separated itself from the rest and waddled toward a far corner. Even drenched in blood, I recognized the grizzled object in its mouth. It was one of the farmer's arms. Or, had been, at least. It was now only a ragged piece of meat. Food for a savage beast.

The slamming of a screen door finally stole my attention from the macabre scene. A tiny old woman shuffled her way down the porch steps. Clutched in her hands was a long, double-barrel shotgun. The moonlight glinted off its deep finish. Her gait was fraught with age as she made her way toward me.

I took a step back before realizing that, even though she was headed in my direction, she wasn't coming for me. With her eyes telegraphing her intent, she made a beeline for the pen. She bore down on the pigs like a wolf stalking a scent.

I could only assume it had been her husband's screams that had brought her out.

"Earl, you son of a bitch!" The woman stepped up to the pen and peeked through the middle and top rail. She raised the shotgun, prepared to fire. A moment later, she dropped it to her side in disappointment. It was too late. The woman looked at me a moment before turning back to the pigpen. "The son of a bitch threatened to do it. Didn't think he'd go through with it so soon."

"So..." The words didn't want to come out. I didn't want to believe their meaning. "So, he *did* do it on purpose!"

"Of course, he did, the old coot. Times are tough 'round here. About to lose the farm, we is. That insurance money, God rest his soul, couldn't come at a better time, though."

"You mean..."

"Still, the son of a bitch coulda had the decency to tell an old woman goodbye. Fifty-three years I gave him."

The old woman stepped back from the railing. Pulling a crucifix from inside the top of her blouse, she kissed it then tucked it back in. Noticing the camera resting idly in my trembling hands, the woman gestured toward me with the barrel of her shotgun. "Well, don't just stand there. Get some photographs so we have somethin' to show the investigators."

And there it was.

The camera remained cradled where it was, chest-high. I couldn't raise it further. I couldn't bring myself to do as she asked. Or, as the old farmer had wished, apparently. I didn't have it in me. I had neither the strength, nor the resolve for such a task.

Releasing a deep sigh, the old woman slung the shotgun over her shoulder. "Well, that's that, I reckon." She shot one last glance into the pen, blew a kiss in its general direction, then turned back to me. She let out a deep breath. "You may as well come into the house and have some supper while I make the phone call."

I looked at the woman wide-eyed. I had to force my mouth to work. "Ma'am, I can't eat!" I held my stomach like that would hold in its contents. "Not after what I just saw. Not after…" *Holy shit!* I still couldn't believe what I had just seen. Putting it into words proved even more difficult.

"Well, shoot." The woman's disappointment showed in the creases of her moonlit face. "Can't let it go to waste. That pork butt is the last of her."

I took one last look in the pen. The frenzy had quelled. Only the sounds of bone and gristle being chewed by powerful jaws remained.

"Her?"

"Ol' Penelope."

I gaped at the woman who'd just lost her husband in horrific fashion and was hardly reacting accordingly.

"Who gives a shit about some old pig?!"

"We did, that's who. Why, she's the one that ate our son, God rest his soul." The old woman turned and started trudging toward the house. Over the fading sounds of natural selection, I heard her mutter, "Damned if that check didn't go as far as we thought it would."

The Dark Side

"Ya know, a lady disappeared in one of these a few years ago." Brent's face shows no sign of jest. Even when he's bullshitting, he has the knack for playing it straight.

"Oh, I'm sure." Fortunately, Sky has the knack for sniffing out Brent's bullshit. "And I bet she hasn't been heard from since."

Brent's eyes widen, taking on a look of surprise. "So, you've heard the story!"

Sky slaps her boyfriend on the shoulder. "I'm already doing this under protest. If you're trying to scare me, it's not gonna help your cause." Sky checks her watch. "Besides, I'm breaking curfew for this, and the new dorm mother gets off on handing out red cards. It's like she's trying to meet a quota or something. After tonight, I'm sure I'll have one."

Brent pulls a shiny, silver flask from inside his jacket pocket. "Maybe this will help." Shielding it from the eyes of those in line behind them, Brent unscrews the cap from the slim container and nudges it in Sky's direction.

After a quick glance around, Sky takes both the flask

and a sip. She has yet to acquire a love for the piney taste of gin, but the night is crisp and she is without coffee to keep her warm. Besides, if there was anything she learned from her mother it was that nothing takes the edge off like liquor. Taking a second pull from the flask, she can hear her doctor's warning about mixing her prescription with alcohol. She drowns the voice in her head with another drink.

She hands the flask back to Brent who tilts it back and takes a pull.

On the car ride to the blackout house, he had spelled out exactly what they were in for this evening. He explained all about blackout houses and how, like escape rooms, the attraction was gaining in popularity. The inability to see while trying to find your way from entrance to exit makes for an even more unnerving and psychologically frightening experience. A challenge for those looking to test themselves beyond aimlessly wandering through a simple haunted house.

It is that inability to see that is reason enough for Sky to be hesitant. The loss of faculties is hardly an anxiety sufferer's friend. Her suggestion that they attend a midnight showing of Rocky Horror at The Drexel, or even hosting a horror film marathon in her dorm as alternatives to the blackout house, had been met with derision. Brent wasn't about to be deterred. He is as excited about his first blackout experience as a kid about to attend her first boy/girl birthday party.

The name of this particular blackout house is The Dark Side. Situated between a haunted schoolhouse and a nuclear factory overrun with zombies, the trio of makeshift buildings have been temporarily erected on the county fairgrounds for the Halloween season. While her deep-rooted relationship with anxiety means haunted attractions are hardly on Sky's list of fun things to do, they are most certainly on Brent's. If she hadn't come along, he would have come anyway. Most likely with his frat brothers, and who knows what drunken trouble they would have gotten into? She refuses even to imagine. It is definitely better that Sky is with him. For both their sakes.

"Ladies and gentleman! Welcome to The Dark Side!"

The barker walking up and down the line is dressed in a priest's robe and collar. A partially concealed devil's tail hangs out of the back. Sky questions the duality, but doesn't expel much effort. It is, after all, Halloween and that means all bets are off.

"Inside the world's most terrifying blackout house, you may encounter spirits. You may encounter a maniac or two. You may even encounter things you thought only existed in nightmares. What you will *not* encounter, however, is an easy way out. There is but one exit, and it is at the end. Ladies and gentlemen, The Dark Side is not for the faint of heart."

The priest's spiel is over-rehearsed and over-exaggerated as he strolls up and down the line. For those waiting to enter the attraction, he does his best to work them into a frothy mass of rabid excitement. For those not so sure they made the right decision, the monologue has a different affect: girlfriends clutch tighter to the arms of their dates; once brave, but now wide-eyed pre-teens move a step closer to their parents.

At some point, Sky stops listening to the priest, forcing his scare tactics to the back of her mind like so much white noise. She isn't excited in the least, and certainly doesn't need to be worked into a frothy mass. She tries not to let on, but her stomach is already in knots.

"Anyone who wishes to enter The Dark Side," the priest continues, "will be required to sign a waiver,"

This gets Sky's attention. *Waiver?* She looks to Brent, her raised eyebrows seeking explanation.

"It's just a formality," Brent says. "A, it legally lets them off the hook if some jackass freaks out and runs head first into a wall."

A trio of young women make their way passed. They have just exited the blackout house and it shows on their faces. One of the ladies uses a tissue to wipe away tears running down her cheeks. The second young lady stares straight ahead with dead, shell-shocked eyes. The third gleefully types away on her cell phone. Her eyes are alive. A smile graces her face. Sky hears her say something about doing it again as they pass.

The nail on Sky's thumb enters her mouth. "And B?"

Brent shrugs. "It's just another way to scare you, babe. To make you think something truly dangerous is waiting inside."

Sky's eyes narrow.

"It's not a big deal." Brent rubs Sky's arm. "They can't hurt you. Can't touch you. It's just a big, dark maze." He offers Sky the flask. "Want another?"

Shaking her head, Sky turns away. Her teeth begin working on her thumbnail. The man in line behind her looks as if he is about to be sick. His friend laughs and claps him on the back. Sky wonders how many people in line really don't want to be here.

As the priest makes his way toward them, Sky must try harder to ignore him; a task made more difficult as he stops right in front of her. When their eyes meet, he peers deep into hers. "And that's when you'll be given this evening's safe word."

Sky's jaw drops, releasing her thumb. "Safe word?"

The priest hears her, has to, but doesn't respond. With the prideful smile of a job well done, he spins on his heels and continues toward the front of the line. His pointed devil's tail sways back and forth in his wake.

Sky turns on her boyfriend of four months.

"Bullshit, Brent!" She keeps her voice low, but makes her irritation known. "A safe word? Seriously?"

"Babe." Brent slips the flask back into his jacket. He wraps his arms around Sky. "Again, it's just another way to up the fear factor. It's fine, I swear. It's what they do. Just relax."

Despite how much logic Brent dishes out, Sky has all but made up her mind that she isn't about to relax. Probably couldn't even if she wanted to. Like it or not, anxiety is her cross to bear. *Embrace it,* her mother had once said, speaking as someone tormented by her own mental demons. *It's what reminds us we're alive.* But if her mother had spent more time seeking help and less time believing her everyday dreams were premonitions, she might still be alive.

Brent shuffles forward as the line moves.

Sky reluctantly follows.

The closer she gets to the entrance, the more Sky can hear the occasional scream erupting from inside the blackout house. And the more she calls bullshit on Brent's claim that nothing more than a simple maze awaits them inside.

"Getting excited?"

It is as if Brent doesn't know her at all.

"More like getting prepared." She tries to sound just the right amount of irritated.

Ten minutes later, Sky and Brent step up to the table just outside the entrance to the blackout house. A woman in a blood-splattered nurse's uniform sits behind the table. The costume is one of those low cut white uniforms that is supposed to be sexy and shows a disturbing amount of cleavage. The woman smiles at Sky and Brent as if they are in for great fun and she is excited on their behalf. Sky feels her anxiety creep up a notch.

"Hey, you two," the faux nurse says. She slides two half-sheet pieces of paper in front of them. "Need you to sign these waivers, then we'll get you inside."

Sky wastes no time. "What's the safe word?"

Brent laughs as he leans down and picks up a pen. "Jesus, babe. Just sign the waiver. We'll get the safe word, don't worry."

Sky ignores Brent's condescension and picks up the sheet of paper. The cover of night works in the attraction owners' favor. Other than the neon sign of a nearby corn dog vendor, the only light comes from the tall, temporary lighting positioned every so often on the grounds. While it is adequate enough for standing in lines, it makes the lettering on the waiver hard to read. Most people probably just signed the paper without trying to read it. But Sky won't be swayed so easily, and the nurse apparently notices.

"It's nothing too serious, hun." The nurse leans forward, further accentuating her bosom. She picks up the sheet Brent has just scribbled his name on. "Just states that you can't sue the owners of the attraction or the fair-grounds for any injuries you might sustain while inside the blackout house." She smiles and drops her voice to a more intimate level. "But, I'm not even sure it would hold up in court, to be honest."

Sky looks at Brent. He returns the nurse's smile, holds it too long. His eyes are practically glued to the woman's cleavage. Sky digs the heal of her sneaker into the top of his foot. His smile vanishes.

The nurse lays Brent's waiver on top of a pile already on the table and leans back in her seat. "But don't worry, hun. I've worked these things for years, and I haven't seen anyone hurt, yet."

The nurse's smile and wink comfort Sky, but only slightly. Her rattled nerves are beyond the point of verbal persuasion.

Sky picks up the pen and exhales deeply. There is no backing out now. Not that she would. Brent would never forgive her.

When Sky finally puts pen to paper, it comes as no surprise that the ink is red. As she signs her name, the phrase "written in blood" comes to mind, and she assumes that's the point. She shakes her head. *What haven't these people thought of?*

"Alright!" No sooner has Sky finished the "n" in "Warren" when Brent snatches the pen from her. Grabbing her by the arm, he not-so gently coaxes her toward the entrance. "Let's do this!"

A tall dark-skinned man stands beside the entrance. He is dressed in the attire of a voodoo shaman. The tails of his black coat hit him just behind the knees. He wears a wicked, yet playful smile and tips back his top hat, further revealing his painted white face. Pinched between his thumb and forefinger is a thick, dark cigar, the end of which glows a bright orange. His eyes are wild with excitement. They sparkle with the aid of nearby neon. "Looks like you're next!"

"Yay." Sky infuses as much sarcasm as possible. "So excited."

Brent laughs. Her tendency to lean on sarcasm as a coping mechanism is a personality trait he doesn't always appreciate, so it's nice that he does this time. "Come on, babe. We're doing this, so you might as well enjoy yourself."

Sky slumps on the inside. Off the top of her head, she

can think of ten other activities in which she would indeed enjoy herself. Her hopes aren't high for the blackout house.

"Should you require it," the shaman says, "this evening's safe word is 'creole.'"

Fitting. Sky commits the word to memory. She doubts Brent does the same. She can practically hear him roll his eyes in ridicule.

"Why, thank you, good sir." Brent pretends to tip his own invisible hat. "But, I don't think we'll be needing the safe word tonight."

The tall man smiles and tips his hat in return.

Brent slides his hand down Sky's arm and takes her by the hand. "Ready?"

Sky considers a last-ditch effort to run. It is truly now or never. "As ready as I'll ever be, I guess."

Brent smiles. "That's the spirit."

A second later, Brent steps through the gaping doorway that is The Dark Side's entrance, pulling Sky along behind him. The room they enter is blacker than a starless night. A black curtain falls behind them, cutting them off from the rest of the world.

"Shit." Sky feels a chill crawl up her back. She waves her hand in front of her face, but might as well have not even tried. She now knows why the attraction is fittingly called a blackout house. It is a much better, and more precise name than "really dark house" or even "difficult to see house." Sky shakes her head at the ridiculousness of her neurotic thoughts. She also knows the chances are good that there will be more.

Beside her in the darkness, Brent chuckles. "You're fine." He clutches her hand a little tighter. "We're in this together. And hey, I bet we make it through in record time."

Despite his encouraging words, the fact that Brent's

voice is no longer so upbeat is not lost on Sky. For the first time in the week since he brought up the idea of the blackout house, he doesn't sound entirely excited. Pensive would be a better word for it. Sky assumes the reality of how much fun this whole thing *won't* be is finally hitting him.

As for Sky, it hit her before they even pulled into the parking lot.

She matches Brent step for step, shuffle for shuffle, doing her best to remain at his side. She uses her free hand to search the darkness for a wall, door, anything tangible. The Dark Side is silent for the moment.

"We must be in a big, open room 'cause I'm not feeling a thing. You?"

Sky shakes her head in response, then remembers Brent can't see her. Her silence will have to be answer enough as she focuses on slowing her elevated heart rate. Her nerves are getting the better of her. She starts thinking just how stupid blackout houses are. A haunted house, maybe. While not her cup of tea, she can see how they could possibly be fun. Especially the cheesier ones where the gore is so over the top, it can't possibly be real. But this? Stumbling around in a pitch-black house with no direction or sense of where to go is just asinine. She has already determined that The Dark Side will be both her first and her last—

Something grazes Sky's shoulder.

She gasps. A shriek scales up her throat, but she doesn't let it escape. A hundred scenarios flood her mind, none of which come as a comfort. She draws up against Brent, compresses herself against his athletic form.

"Jesus, Brent." Sky buries her face in his shoulder. "Something just brushed up against me." Her voice quivers, but she no longer gives a damn. All thoughts of hiding her fear went out the window the second she realized they weren't alone in the room.

"Shh. Okay." Brent's voice is soft and gentle, but his actions are not. Shifting gears, he moves to his immediate right, taking Sky with him. "Let's get the hell out of this room."

He says the words like doing so will bring about the end of their ordeal; like bright lights, colorful streamers and smiles await them in the next room. Sky knows better. Beyond this room lies only more of the same.

Darkness.

Unknown.

After taking only a few steps in the new direction, Brent abruptly stops.

Sky clings tight to his side, reaches out her hand. A sharp intake of air.

They've found a wall.

"Which way?"

When Brent doesn't answer right away, Sky assumes he is trying to come up with some logical reason for choosing one direction over the other. As if there is one. Pitch black space stretches out to either side.

"Okay," Brent says, "let's keep going to the right. If we go more than a few—" A sharp intake of breath steals the rest of the sentence. "Shit!"

Sky's heart leaps into her throat. "What?"

Brent's breaths come more rapidly, more pronounced. "Something just brushed against my leg!"

The icy finger of terror traces the length of Sky's spine. Hairs stand on her neck. "Dammit, Brent!"

"I know, I know." Brent once again pulls Sky by the hand. "Come on, let's go."

They feel their way along the wall, the shuffling of their feet making the only sound. Sky holds onto each breath until she can't any longer. She is fearful of drawing more attention to their location.

"Here we go." Brent stops so short this time that Sky collapses against him.

"What is it?" Even as the question passes her lips, she isn't sure she wants an answer. Comparatively speaking, the unknown can sometimes be a good thing.

Sometimes.

"It's a door." Brent's breathing is heavy with excitement.

Sky's heart races. The door could very well mean the way out of the room. Most likely did. It also means they have reached the next phase of the blackout house. Only more uncertainty lies ahead.

What if it proves worse?

Sky picks at her teeth with a fingernail. "Do we dare open it?"

For the longest time, Brent doesn't answer. Sky can hear the soft scraping sound of his hand exploring the door.

"Probably can't get out if we don't."

"But what if—"

A low, guttural growl comes from somewhere in the darkness.

Sky's question dies in her throat. She spins, placing her back against the wall. "Brent!"

"I know," he says. His voice is shaky. "I heard it."

The growl comes again, this time louder. This time closer.

And this time, Sky screams.

"I say yes." Urgency infests Brent's voice. "Hell yes, we're opening the door!"

The soft click of a latch echoes through the dark. A

squeal and subsequent groan follow. The sounds of a door opening against its will.

"There is a problem, though."

Sky's heart sinks. Given their current situation, she doesn't want to imagine what would constitute a "problem."

"It's a small door," Brent continues. "Low to the ground. We'll have to crawl through, one at a time."

"Whatever gets us out of here."

His breath tickles Sky's ear as Brent leans in. He keeps his voice low as people often do when delivering bad news. "I'll have to let go of your hand."

Sky's reaction is immediate. The word "no" resonates in her mind. Until Brent said the words out loud, the thought hadn't occurred to her. One at a time means separation. The last thing Sky wants right now is to be separated from Brent. She is also aware of the alternative.

As if reading her mind, Brent's voice comes to her from the dark. "Remember, babe, this is all in fun. I know it's scary. Hell, I'm a little scared. But that's the fun of it. The adrenaline rush. Just remember, there's truly nothing in this room that can or will hurt us."

"And the..." She is hesitant to speak of it aloud, as if acknowledging whatever is making that sound will serve as an invitation to approach. "The growling?"

"Most likely, it's someone with night vision goggles," says Brent. "And a recording device."

Most likely.

"Isn't that right?" Brent shouts. His question echoes in the void.

"Brent!" Sky isn't prepared for the sudden outburst. She slaps at Brent's shoulder with one hand while still clutching him with the other. "Don't do that."

Deep down, Sky knows he is right. And she hates it.

Not because she has a problem with Brent being right, but because she is playing into every damsel in distress stereotype. How disappointed her mother would be.

Sky groans and reluctantly slides her hand out of the comfort of Brent's.

A muffled shriek pierces the quiet. It sends a current down Sky's spine and her hand over her mouth. Best she can tell, the scream came from a nearby room somewhere within the blackout house. Laughter soon follows. It doesn't relieve the tension that grips her shoulders. It only solidifies the fact that more terrors await beyond this room.

"It's just temporary." Brent's voice brings her back to the here and now. His timing never better. "Now who's going first?"

Sky once again starts chewing her thumbnail.

"Shouldn't you? I mean, seems the gentlemanly thing to do." Sky's logic seems perfectly rational in her mind. Though, this time she isn't sure her sarcasm plays the way she intends. With Brent, one never knows.

"I could," Brent says. "But then, who's gonna stop someone from grabbing you from behind?"

The thought causes a wave of dread to wash over her. *Ya know, a lady disappeared in one of these a few years ago.*

"I mean, I won't be able to watch your rear if I go first." As Brent's voice rises above a whisper, Sky knows what's coming. "And you know how much I like watching your rear."

Even in the darkness, Sky knows that Brent is smiling. He isn't lying. Her rear end has been a fixation for Brent since the night they met at The Red Door. They danced until last call that night at the club, and more often than not, either Brent's eyes or hands rested squarely on her rear end.

Her own smile starts to form, but fades as Sky remembers the decision she must make. Go first, or follow. Both options pose equally unsatisfactory results. Be the first to encounter whatever lay ahead? Or be the tag along who gets grabbed from behind without the person in front knowing.

The hungry growl forces Sky's hand from somewhere in the room.

"Okay. I'll go first." Even in the pitch-black, Sky uses her finger to emphasize her point. "But you better stay behind me. And I mean *right* behind me."

"Wouldn't wanna be anywhere else."

With some guidance from Brent, Sky finds the opening. The hole in the wall is roughly the size of a bedroom window—just large enough to crawl through—and low to the ground. Sky works her way into a crouch, then lowers herself onto her hands and knees. She peers into the space, but it does little good. Where they are going is just as dark as where they are. She takes a deep breath, holds it to stall, then sets it free. "Okay. Let's go."

Without further hesitation, Sky crawls through the opening.

Even in the dark, Sky can sense the limitations of her confinement. When she raises her head even a few inches, it bumps the roof of the tunnel. Because despite hopes to the contrary, that is exactly where she finds herself: a tunnel. The tiny opening did not lead directly to another room.

"Brent?" Her voice echoes off the walls.

"Right behind you, babe."

The sound of Brent's voice offers at least some amount of comfort. Sky wills her breaths to come slow and steady as she begins inching herself forward on hands and knees. The air around her quickly turns thick and earthy. The first beads of sweat break along her temples as she continues to crawl deeper into The Dark Side.

She has gone only a few feet when Sky notices just how quiet her surroundings have become. No more screams have erupted from within the blackout house. No growls. And it is then that Sky realizes she has not heard any other shuffling other than her own inside the narrow passageway.

She stops cold.

"Brent?"

Continued silence greets her.

"Brent!" Sky's voice cracks. Her throat is dry. "This isn't funny. Not one damn bit."

Still no answer from the darkness.

Sky's mind splits in twenty directions. Her heart rate soars. It is too soon to panic, but it patiently waits to take control.

"Brent! Damn it, where are you?"

With her chest pounding and adrenaline urging her to make a move, Sky decides to back track. She tries to turn around in the tight space, but is unable. She begins crawling in reverse. Within a second, her feet slam against something hard. The narrow opening she entered only minutes ago is gone. A door, she imagines, now seals off the tunnel, eliminating any chance at retreat. She thrusts a foot backward, kicking the door as hard as she can. A hollow, metallic echo rings out. The pain that shoots up her shin is not worth the effort.

"Brent!"

Full on panic takes the reins. The sweat on Sky's face turns cold. Fear propels her forward into the abyss. Almost instantly, her head slams against something that hadn't been there a moment before. Sky uses a hand to investigate. Once again, a barrier of some type blocks her progress. *Another door? A wall?* It hardly matters. The effect is the same. Sweat drips into her eyes as she finds herself fighting for air. It is then that the horrifying reality of her situation sinks in:

I'm boxed in!

A soft whimper escapes her lips. Trembling hands frantically search her surroundings. Everywhere they go, every direction they probe, they touch the same smooth, metal walls.

"No, no, no, no, no…"

Sky begins slapping at the metal walls. The sound echoes in the tight space, hurting her ears. Her eyes well up and soon tears join the sweat running down her face. Panic grips her like a body suit a size too small. Sky pleads with herself to remain calm. It takes a moment, but her body starts to comply. Taking command of her breaths, she releases each one a little slower, a little more measured. She isn't running out of air just yet, despite what her anxiety tells her. There will be plenty if she simply calms down and conserves it.

Think, girl. Think.

A sound comes from above. It is unmistakable. Suddenly, calming herself becomes a forgotten relic of an idea. The hollow drumming, like dirt being shoveled onto a coffin, reverberates within the space. It is a sound she has heard at funerals numerous times.

Though never from the inside.

One after another, the muffled thrum of earth raining down onto the metal box fills her ears. Pebbles and clods tumble down the sides. In between each cascade, the distant sound of laughter can be heard. It isn't just any laughter. It is familiar and comes from the unmistakable, gravelly voice of the voodoo shaman who greeted them at the entrance. Sky pictures the man standing over the box with shovel in hand, the cigar clenched squarely between his teeth. His wild eyes sparkle as he bends to scoop another load.

It rains down upon the box.

"Stop!" Sky's voice is hoarse. Her throat resembles coarse sandpaper. She can hardly swallow. "Please!" The heat inside the box rises. "Help me! There's somebody in here!" A thought comes to her, and not a moment too soon. "Creole! Creole!"

Another load of dirt rains down.

The laughter increases in volume. It grows more robust. It's a suggestive laugh and turns Sky's blood cold. Upon the box, one load of dirt after another falls.

A sudden popping noise. It is the sharp crumpling of metal. Sky feels the roof of the box buckle until it presses against the top of her head. She must crouch even further. The metal pops again, this time louder. The buckling of the roof soon forces Sky against the floor of the box. The weight from each shovel full of dirt steals even more of Sky's already limited space. For the first time, pain registers in her legs from being bent awkwardly beneath her. There is nowhere left to go. The roof presses firmly against her back.

The safe word once again enters her thoughts, but Sky finds she can no longer call out. Her lungs can't draw in the required air. She doubts it would even matter. All she can do now is let the tears come. And wait. For what, she has no idea. Ultimately, she sees only two possible outcomes: the walls could suddenly fly open, releasing her into a room filled with smiling people asking if she'd had the time of her life, or…

She tries not to think of the other outcome.

And then it happens. Her worst fear is realized. A loud crack emanates from above. The metal roof over Sky's head splits at the seams. A moment later, it completely gives way, collapsing on top of her. Dirt quickly fills the voids around her. Within seconds, all empty space is taken up with musty earth. Silence taunts as Sky struggles to breathe. She presses her face into the crook of her elbow. A small pocket of air. She fears it is the last she will ever breathe. She sips it sparingly.

Minutes pass. Her thoughts must make their way through the oncoming fog. She can't shake it off.

Sky teeters on the edge of unconsciousness when something in the darkness tickles her ankle. Instinctively, she jerks her leg, but can't move it far. The sensation teases her skin a second time. Sky screams as best she can, but what comes out can hardly be classified as such. Damp soil finds its way passed her lips and into her mouth. The sour taste of moss turns her stomach.

Whatever tickled her ankle now crawls up her pant leg. She tries to kick it off and is once again denied. The sensation makes its way up her calf.

Something crawls along the base of her neck. By frantically moving her head back and forth, Sky is able to work her arm up through darkness. Dirt immediately fills the chasm, pilfering her air supply. As something weaves its way through her hair, she tries brushing it away with her fingers. She succeeds only in chasing the culprit down her neck and into the collar of her sweatshirt, well beyond her reach.

Sky tries to pull her hand away and finds the task more difficult than it should be. Her hand is caught in her hair. Only it isn't hair that entwines her fingers. When she finally tears her hand free, silky cobwebs cling to her fingers.

The spiders seem to multiply. They are on her body and in her hair. Her mind screams where her throat cannot. The air in the space decreases as the heat continues to rise. Sky gasps for breath. Perspiration now sheets her entire body. Her clothes cling to her. Dirt clings to her clothes. She spits moist earth from her tongue. The spiders tip-toe over her body.

Crushed beneath the weight and mounting dread, Sky starts to break down. Tears flow unimpeded. Breaths come in short, inadequate bursts, yet she hasn't the strength to fight for more. She is devoid of bravery and ready to admit defeat. The shaman has won. The blackout house has won. She has lost. Whatever fate has decided, she is ready to give in. Then, with a sudden awareness and ache in her chest, she realizes she already has.

"Sky?"

The voice is faint and far away, but recognizable. It takes only a moment to realize she has heard this voice every day for months. It is a comforting voice. It is Brent's voice.

The sobs cease, but the tears take longer. Sky briefly forgets the spiders that are busy making her body their new home. With the only sensory she still has at her disposal, Sky seeks out the voice. After several seconds, all she can hear is the continued tittering of tiny legs. Is that a symptom of the end, hearing the voices of loved ones? And how far gone will her mind be when the end finally comes? As she contemplates the relief that death will bring, she hears the voice again.

"Sky?"

This time, her name comes from somewhere close. Somewhere in the darkness. What remains of her spirit cries out, begs to be found. Suddenly, hope is a possibility that is allowed.

Sky tries to call out, but her voice continues to fail. Her throat is so ravaged and constricted, little more than an exhaustive surge of stale air ekes out. A spider makes its way across her cheek, and she is forced to clamp her mouth shut.

The sliver of hope slips away. She senses the warmth enveloping her more than she feels it. Is it her imagination? Or is this death's embrace from which the saying comes?

"Sky!"

When her eyes spring open, a bright light shines from overhead. Neon surrounds her. Sky gasps for air, and when she opens her mouth, dirt does not enter. Cool autumn air fills her lungs. Her arms flail outward. She can move. Gone is the box that held her captive. Gone is the dirt. She stands at the table near the entrance to The Dark Side, her heart racing. Sky reaches up and runs a trembling hand through her hair. It comes away free and clear. The spiders are gone.

Across the table, the woman dressed as a nurse eyes her with a wrinkled brow.

"Babe." Brent has a hold of her arm. He shakes it gently. "Hey, you okay? You kinda zoned out on me there."

With her chest heaving, Sky looks down at the piece of paper on the table before her. Her name is emblazoned in red. She looks at the pen still gripped in her hand. Sky lays it down and takes a step back from the table.

"No—"

"Alright!" Brent exclaims. "Let's do this!"

With his hand still clutching her arm, Brent urges Sky toward the entrance to the blackout house. The doorway, a large heinous rectangle of darkness, beckons her. But what awaits Sky on the other side of that rectangle terrifies her.

"Wait!" But her feet fall in line with Brent's as she shuffles toward the entrance. She has no control. A couple more steps and they are only inches from the door.

"Looks like you're next," says a tall, dark-skinned man

standing beside the entrance. He is dressed in the attire of a voodoo shaman. He wears a wicked, yet playful smile and tips back his top hat, further revealing his painted white face. The end of his cigar glows a bright orange. His eyes are wild with excitement and sparkle with the aid of nearby neon. "You know, a lady disappeared in one of these a few years ago." He tips his hat. "In you go!"

"Wait!" Despite her shouts, it is as if nobody is listening. Brent's grip on Sky's arm remains firm, pulling her along. The doorway greets them. "Wait!" she shouts again. "Safe word! What's the safe word?"

As she is pulled through the doorway, Sky turns her head and looks outward. The last thing she sees is the smile of the tall man. It is no longer a smile of greeting, but a smile of contempt. Contempt for whom, she does not know. And she never is given the safe word.

Growing Cold Together

"First name will have to be good enough." Kyle looked down at the steaming yellow letters in the white snow and chuckled. "Catch frostbite if I leave him out any longer." Kyle shook, tucked, then zipped his fly. He blew hot air into his hands and looked toward the woods. Unlike Kyle, his fiancé was apparently either too bashful or too refined to pee on the shoulder of the road, choosing instead to find that perfect tree. He had hoped to see her making her way back toward the road by now.

She wasn't.

"Angelique! Babe! Move that sweet, tanned ass of yours!" Kyle's words echoed through the trees before returning to him.

It had been hard enough getting her to agree to a ski trip in Colorado. Being from Panama, Angelique was more of a flip-flops, cut off jean shorts and a bikini top kind of girl and not so much snow boots and ski coat. Though she looked good in both.

Kyle leaned against the front of his GMC Denali and dug into the pocket of his North Face coat. He pulled out what was left of the joint he and Angelique had started before stopping to piss. Placing it between his lips, he lit the end. Kyle tilted his head back and blew ringlets of marijuana smoke into the moonlit night. The skunky scent mixed with the cold air that tickled his cheeks. The last he'd seen, the thermometer on the dashboard had read twelve degrees. It was supposed to drop further overnight.

"What the hell is taking her?"

"Keep your pants on," Gabriela said, emerging from the back seat of the SUV. "She'll be done when she's done."

Kyle sometimes wished Gabriela's English wasn't so good. This trip was one of those times.

Angelique's older sister was a sworn pain in Kyle's ass. And a consolation prize; the carrot he'd hung in front of Angelique to convince her to come on the trip. To sweeten the deal. If he'd had his way, they wouldn't have even told the older woman where they were going, much less brought her along. Unlike Kyle's parents, Angelique's were still alive. But they lived in Panama. Gabriela was the only family Angelique had in the States. The two were inseparable, like peanut butter and jelly. Eggs and bacon. Chips and guac.

Damned if the munchies weren't already kicking in.

"It's been a long drive." Kyle inhaled, held it for a moment, let it out. "I'd like to reach the lodge before midnight."

Gabriela didn't say anything. Shaking her head, she walked around to the rear of the SUV.

"Don't go far," he called after her. "I'm not waiting around on you, too."

Kyle couldn't see her, but he knew his future sister-in-law well. Gabriela's middle finger was most likely raised in his direction. It was her way of showing how little she appreciated him and everything he has done for her. Kyle didn't know why Gabriela disliked him so much. He treated Angelique well. Loved her. Doted on her. It was a mystery.

Regardless, Kyle welcomed Gabriela's exit. Not to mention the fresh air. The woman wore enough cheap perfume to choke roadkill. A road trip "don't" if there ever was one. Her perfume would linger in the Denali's interior long after the smell of weed was gone.

"Babe! Come on!"

A minute later, Angelique still hadn't emerged from the woods. Kyle wasn't too concerned just yet. At least not about anything more than getting to the lodge, stripping down and kicking back in front of the fire with his girl. The frigid outside temperature demanded layers of clothing, but he couldn't wait to get Angelique inside and out of hers. The radiance from her tanned skin alone would be enough to thaw out anyone.

Kyle determined she had been gone for at least fifteen minutes.

He couldn't wait any longer.

"I'm gonna see what's keeping her." He wasn't sure if Gabriela could hear him, and it really didn't matter. He wasn't about to repeat himself.

"Hold on," Gabriela said, making her way around the rear of the Denali. "You're not leaving me here."

Kyle's heart sank. He shouldn't have said anything. Gabriela appeared at his side before he had taken more than a couple steps.

"Aw, you wanna be close to me," Kyle goaded, zipping his jacket up to his chin. "That's so sweet."

"No, I just don't want to stand out here all night wondering what happened after your dumb ass falls off a cliff."

It was a good comeback, he'd give her that. "Yeah, well," Kyle said, "if we get separated, I'll just follow the smell of my grandmother's perfume. It'll lead me right to you." Kyle shook his head. Would it always be like this between them? He didn't know, but if he had to speculate…

Kyle shook his head and returned his attention to the trek ahead. A snowplow had deposited a two-foot mound of grey snow along the side of the road. It separated the pavement from the forest like a moat.

"I doubt she went far," Kyle said. "Let's go."

Quite literally following in Angelique's smaller, but conveniently-placed footsteps, Kyle navigated the snow bank with Gabriela in his shadow. Even on the other side of the mound, the snow came up well over his ankles. The extra fifty bucks for the boots with the rabbit fur lining was already proving money well spent.

Niveous pine trees, the trunks of which were scalped most of the way up, ascended into the night sky like straws from a large, white snow cone. Their bushy tops meshed together in places, keeping the moon from getting through. Random splotches of light reached the ground only here and there. And where it didn't, the night created a murky and shadowy terrain where anything could hide.

Kyle tried not to think about that too much. He focused instead on following Angelique's tracks. The snow's benefits were two-fold: not only did they provide well-defined evidence of where someone had walked, but the moonlight reflecting off of the fresh blanket of white kept the night from being dangerously dark.

"You shouldn't have let her go off on her own."

Kyle stopped and looked at Gabriela like that was the dumbest comment he had heard in a while. "Let her? Like anyone can control that woman." He shrugged and started walking. "She said she couldn't piss by the road, so…"

"You know there are more than twenty-four million acres of nothing but wilderness out there, right?"

Kyle looked at his future sister-in-law. "Since when are you an expert on Colorado landscape?"

"I can read," Gabriela said. "What do you think I've been doing back there this whole trip while you two are all baby talk and kissy face?"

Entering the forest, two things became immediately evident: not only was Kyle out of shape, but keeping the altitude and cold from stealing the air from his lungs was going to be a struggle. It was downright hypothermic up on the mountain.

Kyle and Gabriela started up the slight incline. Steam rose from their breaths. Snow crunched beneath their boots. When Kyle looked back at the shrinking Denali, its black silhouette was nearly shielded by tree trunks. They had already come further than he thought. Kyle wondered again why Angelique had come so far into the woods just to piss. He loved her modesty. It sometimes made him chuckle.

This wasn't one of those times.

"An-gel-i-que!" Gabriela's sing-song call pinballed through the trees.

If Angelique heard, she didn't respond.

Just ahead, the footprint pattern changed. The impressions were spaced farther apart, their forms not quite so neat. To Kyle's untrained eye, it appeared as if Angelique had started running. From what, he didn't know. Maybe an animal had frightened her. An unfamiliar sound. But why not head back toward the road?

Gabriela came up and stood beside Kyle. "What is it?"

Kyle exchanged a glance, then turned his attention further up the trail.

"I don't know," he said. "Let's go." Kyle trudged onward. He didn't want to tell Gabriela that her sister may have gotten turned around and that was why she had taken off further into the woods. It was the only explanation Kyle could come up with. And it didn't bode well. There was no telling how far they would have to follow her tracks before finally meeting up with Angelique.

It was not far.

Just as suddenly as the footprints had changed, they came to an abrupt end. Even in the darkness, Kyle recognized the smear of blood at the base of a large, and apparently very old pine tree. The varied shades of red were due to concentrations and stood out like spilled paint against the white canvas. It was an unfortunate, yet easy distinction to make.

Kyle doubled over and emptied the contents of his stomach.

The scream came from over Kyle's right shoulder. He clasped a hand to his ear as Gabriela emptied her lungs. Long after her throat was spent, the scream lingered in the trees. It made its way deep into the woods and made Kyle feel suddenly vulnerable. Paranoid, even. The marijuana smoke swirling in his head made matters worse.

Kyle turned and threw his arms around his sister-in-law. Another shriek rose up, but he cut it off with a hand over her mouth.

"Shh, dammit!" Kyle spat the whisper directly into Gabriela's ear. "You're freaking me out!"

Truth be told, it wasn't just her, but a combination of the screaming, the blood, and their surroundings. Kyle's head was spinning. His heart pounding. His nerves were ablaze and his now empty stomach roiled.

When he felt it was safe to do so, Kyle slowly removed his hand from Gabriela's mouth. When she remained silent, he gently slid his arms from around her and took a step back.

Gabriela's hand replaced Kyle's. Her voice trembling, she spoke through her fingers. "That's…"

"Yes." Kyle didn't want to hear the words. "It is."

Scattered within the blood-soaked area was a melee of footprints. And not just Angelique's. A struggle had taken place on that spot. With someone or some*thing*.

Kyle's heart sank like a stone in a pond. He visually scoured the area. With the exception of thousands of Colorado's finest lodgepole pines, they appeared alone. But the same couldn't have been said for Angelique. She hadn't been alone and something had happened because of it.

Something very bad.

Guilt hit him square in the chest. Kyle had to fight the urge to run deeper into the woods, screaming Angelique's name. Attracting unwanted attention didn't seem the best play. Not out here. Not now. His focus returned to the blood-soaked snow.

"Is it…" The words struggled to make it passed Gabriela's lips. "Is it hers?"

The forest remained still, their breathing the only sound.

Kyle shook his head. "I don't know." But down deep, his gut told him that he knew all too well. He could only hope that he was wrong, that perhaps the blood hadn't come from his bride-to-be, but some poor bastard of an animal that had met its unfortunate, yet natural end. Maybe an old kill that had been there awhile. Even as the thought entered his mind, the steam rising from the red snow told him that wasn't the case.

The kill was fresh.

"What do we do?"

Kyle had momentarily forgotten about Gabriela standing behind him. Her voice came out so soft and mousy, the fact that it startled him was a testament to how on edge he was.

Kyle breathed warm air into his fist. His chin quivered from both the cold and the implications. He willed himself to be strong, though he felt anything but. His heart was breaking, even if there was no definitive reason for it to just yet. He felt numb all over.

He looked to Gabriela with no good answer to her question. Except for the tears streaming down her frozen cheeks, the woman's face was blank. She looked lost, scared and bewildered all at once. Kyle doubted she would even know her own name if asked. When their eyes met, gone was the spite that usually resided in them. Despair was all that lingered.

Kyle turned away, fighting back tears of his own.

"Our best bet is to go back to the truck. Get my cell phone and call for help." Kyle wiped away water as it escaped his eyes. "We'll have a better chance of finding Angelique with more of us looking."

"Oh, my God!" Gabriela shouted. Her native tongue started flowing in some sort of mantra or prayer.

Kyle's nerves pinged. He spun back. "What? What is it?"

Gabriela's head was tilted back, her wide eyes trained on the treetops. Both hands covered her mouth.

Kyle's natural instinct was to follow her lead. He looked up.

It was a mistake.

Kyle's jaw dropped.

He sucked in a breath. The abrupt intake of cold air stung his throat.

Thirty feet in the air, the woman he'd been ready to love till death hung limp, sprawled out between two large branches. The limbs bowed under her weight. Her head tilted back unnaturally, dead eyes looking toward the ground below. Red covered Angelique's new white, fur-lined ski jacket, spreading down her sleeves. Blood dripped from the cluster of intestines hanging from her torso.

Aghast, Kyle stepped up to the tree. His heart raced. His first impulse was to climb, to get to her. But there were no branches he could reach. He settled for his second impulse.

"Angelique!"

There was no response, save for the screaming that once again erupted from behind him. Gabriela was hysterical. And Kyle couldn't blame her.

A drop of warm blood hit Kyle's frozen cheek. Then another.

His legs buckled.

His stomach churned.

He rested his hand against the tree to keep from collapsing.

Despair washed over him. He wanted to give in to it, but didn't have time. In the canopy of limbs hovering above Angelique, two large, yellow eyes appeared, tucked back in the shadows.

"Are those…" he started to ask. When they blinked, he knew that they were.

A frenzied crunching of snow tore Kyle's attention from the gruesome scene. Gabriela was running, making her way from the tree, the blood, her sister as fast as her footing would allow. Kyle understood the urge. Felt it himself.

The problem was that Gabriela, too, was heading in

the wrong direction. She was running away from the road and the safety of the Denali, not toward it.

"Gabriela!"

But if she heard Kyle's shout, she chose to ignore it. Another few seconds and she would be out of sight. He needed to do something or risk losing track of Gabriela as well.

Kyle gazed once again upon the tree limbs overhead, holding out a sliver of hope that he'd been mistaken. That Angelique's body wasn't nestled in their clutches after all.

No such luck. Angelique remained on her back, limp arms still hanging toward the ground. Only one aspect had changed: the large, yellow eyes that had hovered above her were now gone.

A sound came from the other side of the tree trunk. The subtle packing of snow, followed by animalistic heavy breathing.

And with tears in his eyes and his heart in his throat, Kyle ran.

He followed Gabriela's footprints—high-stepping through the snow—until he could see her up ahead. She hadn't made it far. She was out of breath and slowing down.

By the time Kyle caught up with her, Gabriela had come to a stop beside a snow-covered stump. Only then did he dare shoot a glance behind him. As far as he could tell, nothing was following. Could he trust his watery eyes? Could he trust anything right now?

"Hey," he said. His heavy breathing sent billows of steam into the air.

When Gabriela lifted her head, her face was ashen, completely drained of blood. The combination of exertion and sub-freezing temperatures weren't enough to put color in her cheeks. Tears had frozen on her skin. It created a shine like porcelain. Out of breath and fighting for air, she leaned against the stump for support.

"Did you see?" Gabriela's words came out intermittently, alternating between gulps of air.

Kyle nodded as he raised his hands and placed them atop his head, forcing oxygen into his lungs. He had seen, alright. But he didn't want to talk about it. Didn't think he could just yet. If ever. He focused instead on his newest priority: getting the two of them out of the forest alive. Right now, survival trumped everything else.

Even Angelique.

"You're heading in the wrong direction." Kyle kept his eyes on the landscape behind them. He thought he saw a shadow duck behind a tree a ways back. But the tree trunk was so slim—roughly the size of a roll of paper towels—his eyes must have been playing tricks. Nothing capable of taking down Angelique and carrying her up a tree could hide behind such a thin tree trunk. "You brought us deeper into the woods," he continued. "We need to be heading back that way, towards the road."

Kyle pointed in the direction they'd just come.

Gabriela lifted her eyes. "I'm not going back that way." Snot ran down and over her lip. She wiped it away with her sleeve. "Just leave me here."

Kyle shook his head. "I'm not leaving you." He recognized her trauma and was sympathetic. His initial instinct was to go to Gabriela and comfort her. But he couldn't remember a time when an embrace from him would have ever been welcomed. Besides, he was grieving, too, and still trying to process everything.

"I'm heading toward the road." Kyle blew hot air into his hands. Drawing them up into his sleeves, he looked for an alternate route back to the road, one that wouldn't lead them past the tree that held Angelique's body. *Body?* The word tore at his heart. "And you're coming with me. Angelique would never forgive me."

At the mention of her sister's name, the floodgates opened. Gabriela was soon beside herself with fresh tears.

With equal parts empathy and fear of Gabriela drawing unwanted attention, Kyle knelt in the snow in front of her. He pulled his hands from his sleeves and placed them on her knees. He could feel the frightened woman's legs trembling through her jeans.

"Hey," he said. Only after Gabriela looked up did Kyle continue, their eyes locked on one another. "I've already lost her. We both have. But I'll be damned if we're gonna lose each other. Not tonight. And not out here." His words sounded strange. Kyle had never been one for motivational speaking. Nor had he ever spoken to his sister-in-law with such compassion. But the rules had changed.

Kyle stood.

"So, we need to head back." He cupped his hands over his ears and let his body heat warm them. "But we'll go around the…" Kyle allowed the sentence to trail off, unsure how to describe exactly what it was they wanted to bypass. He was pretty sure, though, that Gabriela knew to what he was referring.

She rose from the stump. Reaching up, Gabriela wiped the blood from Kyle's cheek. "Like, circle our way back?"

"Exactly." Kyle blew heat into his hands again before slipping them back inside his sleeves. The air felt colder. The temperature was falling. "Maybe we go that way. The terrain looks fairly manageable. And when it feels safe, we'll curve back and head south toward the road." Kyle pointed in the direction he was fairly certain would lead them to both the road and the awaiting Denali. Whether or not it was truly south was anyone's guess. It hardly mattered. He could be right or wrong about the direction just as long as he spoke with conviction. One of the few life-lessons his businessman father handed down that he'd actually remembered: Act like you know what you're talking about and people will follow you. Confidence breeds trust.

Kyle was about to cement their bond even further. He was about to give Gabriela an encouraging hug. But something stopped him. It wasn't fear of her reaction or of being rejected. Frankly, he would have been surprised if she had. What stopped him from reaching out to Gabriela was the sound of footsteps in the snow coming from somewhere in the night. It was brief, as if whomever had made the sound immediately realized that it was too loud. The tiny hairs on the back of Kyle's neck came alive.

With the threat of danger rearing its frozen head, all thoughts of empathetic gestures were shelved. Kyle's brain urged him to move, but his body wasn't ready to comply. He didn't know where to go. Every sound in the forest comes as an echo, making it difficult to determine its origin.

Gabriela had heard it, too. She also remained still and allowed her eyes to investigate in silence.

But no other sound came.

The night was still. So was the forest.

"We can't stand here all night," Kyle said. His words were but a whisper. "Especially with the temperature dropping. We need to go."

Gabriela nodded.

Their footsteps were deafening in comparison to the otherwise silent night. The two moved as fast as they could, tromping their way through the snow-covered forest. Each hurried step broadcasted their location to anyone on this side of the mountain. It couldn't be helped. Making noise was a necessary evil if they were to get off the mountain quickly.

Something grabbed the back of Kyle's jacket. He stopped on a dime. Reflex saw him immediately rip his arm away and spin around.

Gabriela stood with her arm outstretched in his direction, her hand clutched in an empty fist. She faced away from Kyle. Her focus was drawn to the trail of footprints they had left behind them.

Short bursts of steam arose from Gabriela's labored breaths.

"What is it?" Kyle turned his eyes from Gabriela to the trail.

"I saw something back there."

Kyle gazed through the sea of slender tree trunks. The mountainous landscape looked the same as anywhere they had been so far. He didn't see anything else. And there wasn't anywhere for anyone or anything to hide. No large rocks, no brush of any sort. Just a white blanket of snow, continually interrupted by tall, skinny pines as far as the darkness allowed.

"There's something back there." Gabriela's voice was steady as she read Kyle's mind. "I saw it. A tall shadow or something. It moved from one tree to another."

Kyle was at a loss. He shrugged. "Which trees?"

Gabriela's face contorted with uncertainty. "I don't know," she said. "They all look the same."

The two remained still and on the lookout for whatever it was that Gabriela thought she had seen. After a minute or two, Kyle gave up on the idea that she had seen anything. More than likely, the distraught and frightened woman just thought she had.

Still, eyes playing tricks or not, something *was* out there. Of that, Kyle was certain. His mind shifted immediately to Angelique. They certainly weren't alone in the forest. She hadn't done that to herself.

"I don't know," he said, wiping fresh tears from his eyes. "I don't see anything. We have to keep mo—"

"Hidebehind."

The whisper was subdued and escaped Gabriela's lips so hushed, Kyle wasn't sure if she was talking to him or to herself.

"Hide behind what?" he asked.

Gabriela shook her head slowly. When she looked up into Kyle's eyes, hers were hooded with reservation. Her bottom lip quivered. Kyle got the sense she was uncertain whether or not to say anything more.

After several seconds had passed, Kyle quit the game. "Forget it. Let's just get—"

"Hidebehind."

"Where, Gabriela?" Kyle tried to keep his growing agitation from infecting his voice. He would need to try harder. "Where do you want us to hide?"

"Not where," Gabriela said, looking around. "It's a what."

Kyle scanned the forest behind them as he awaited further explanation. He still didn't see a damn thing. And they needed to keep moving.

"I read about it," Gabriela continued. "When I was researching the ski lodge and these mountains. It's a…"

Kyle's eyes came back around. "Come on. It's a what?"

"Creature."

"What, like a bear? Mountain lion? There are all kinds of creatures out here, Gabriela."

She shook her head. "Not a regular creature. More of a, what do you call it?" She raised her hands over her head to indicate size. "Big creature. Like a man, but hairy."

Kyle almost chuckled. Was she serious? It wasn't possible. "Bigfoot? Are you saying we're being stalked by Bigfoot?"

"No. But kinda." Gabriela took a quick look around before continuing. "It's called a hidebehind. It's tall. Makes itself thin when it needs to. Sucks in its stomach. It hides behind trees so it can't be seen. Even really, really thin trees."

"But it's as tall as a man?" It was Kyle's turn to shake his head. He started to walk away. They were in real danger here. There was no time for this. "Not possible."

"It kills and eats people in the woods. In *these* woods. A lot of, what are they called? Loggers? It eats their insides."

Kyle stopped, turned and put out his hands. "Okay. Enough. There is no such thing as Bigfoot. Or jackalopes or Tasmanian Devils or Loch Ness fucking Monsters. And I doubt very seriously there is a creature in these woods that can make itself as thin as these trees and wants to eat our insides." His words were sharper than he'd intended, but fear was at the helm now. The clock was ticking. The longer they stood out there...

"Angelique." Tears were streaming down Gabriela's cheeks again. "Explain what happened to her."

Somewhere nearby, a flock of birds ascended from a treetop.

Kyle softened. He fought the urge to picture Angelique's condition and failed. He closed his eyes and allowed the image to come. *The blood. Her body splayed open. Her arms hanging limp. The blood.* He winced. Something had been feasting on Angelique's insides.

Kyle opened his eyes and turned them toward the trail they had blazed behind them.

"Okay." He spoke with his hands as much as anything. "There is definitely something out here with us. I don't know if it's one of those things you're describing or not.

Either way, we can't just stand around waiting for it." Kyle turned to leave. "Come on."

Kyle led the way, with Gabriela following closely behind. Except for the packing of snow, they moved in relative silence. Neither one spoke. Further thoughts of growing fear, the cold and Angelique remained unspoken.

Unspoken, but hard to ignore. Even inside his sleeves, Kyle's hands were frozen. He couldn't feel his fingers and cursed himself for not grabbing his gloves from the Denali. He could see them sitting in the console between the seats. Right beside his cell phone. But who could have guessed they'd be out this long and in need of both? At least the wind wasn't penetrating the trees and making matters worse.

With fatigue hindering their progress, they trudged forward.

When a downed tree blocked their path, it posed both an obstacle and relief. It was the first opportunity they'd had in ten minutes to stop and rest. Kyle looked it up and down, measuring from end to end. The tree stretched a good eighty feet from the bushy top to the uprooted clump of earth that clung to its roots. The fallen pine had to have been one of the area's largest. Going around either end would require a trek of many steps.

"The shortest distance between two points is a straight line, right?"

Kyle threw one leg over the log and then the other. With a little help from the layer of snow, he slid down the backside of the tree with ease. It wasn't until he turned to extend a helping hand to Gabriela that he realized she wasn't there to accept it.

Kyle gasped. "Shit!"

He dropped down, using the log for cover. His head swiveled this way and that. No Gabriela. In fact, there wasn't even a sign that she had ever been with him. The trail behind him was made up of only one set of footprints as far as he could see. Everywhere else, the snow was pristine and untouched. No signs of a struggle. No tell-tail splotches of blood. The trees in this particular area were fewer and farther between. Moonlight penetrated the forest. It provided plenty of light to see by. That wasn't the problem.

Gabriela was simply nowhere to be seen.

It was as if she had just…vanished.

His heart rate jumped up a level. His stomach plummeted. Kyle suddenly felt more vulnerable than ever. More afraid. He resisted the urge to call Gabriela's name. Doing so would let whatever was out there know exactly where he was. But she had been right behind him. Whatever was out there already knew where he was.

Hidebehind.

Had Gabriela simply fallen back?

Why no cry for help?

Why had he not heard *anything*?

A hundred questions flooded his mind as Kyle surveyed the situation from behind the fallen tree. What the hell was out there? Would a bear or mountain lion be that quiet in their attack, that stealth? Kyle didn't think so. Whatever was after them was cautious, calculating. It was as if…it was as if the thing was *playing* with them.

Him, he corrected. Now it was playing with only him.

Unsure what he could do for Gabriela at that point, Kyle had to keep moving. Now more than ever. He was heartsick. He hated leaving Gabriela behind, felt guilty. But once he reached the road and flagged down help, he could send the police to find her.

And retrieve Angelique.

Survival trumped everything.

A rustling of tree branches sounded from overhead. Snow fluttered down. Kyle looked up in time to see a dark shadow pass from one branch to the next. This time, he wasn't seeing things. The tree swayed from the movement. A larger, frozen clump of ice broke free from a limb and fell to the ground. It landed with a thud, narrowly missing him. A smear of red tarnished the white mass.

Kyle scrambled to his feet. Without giving the shadow a second glance, he started running as best he could. The snow was shin-deep and unconducive to haste. He zigged and zagged through the never-ending maze of towering pines. His breaths came quick and labored. Sweat covered his head. His chest ached from both exertion and fear.

He didn't see the ravine until it was too late. One minute he was clomping through the snow, the next, there was no snow. Nor ground beneath it. The cliff's edge caught Kyle's boot, bending his leg behind him as gravity pulled him down the rocky embankment. Instinct made him reach out. He grasped at the jutting rocks for purchase. It failed to slow his decent, but cut and scraped at his hands for the effort. The same rocks, both sharp and blunt, punched at his back. They tore at his ski pants as he slid down the cliff face.

Kyle couldn't help but cry out in pain.

A thin layer of ice and frozen pine needles awaited him at the bottom of the ravine. Kyle's foot broke through and found the sludgy creek bed beneath. The sudden impact sent icy water splashing into the air and a sharp pain ripping up his leg. The water stung Kyle's face. The stream rushed by, wasting no time in finding the top of his boot and making its way inside.

Pulling his foot back through the ice, Kyle hauled himself up onto a sliver of bank running alongside the stream. He rested his back against the rock wall. Adrenaline charged through his racing heart. The shock from the frigid water stole the air from his lungs. Breathing took on the effect of short, interrupted gasps, each one a victory in itself.

You're hyperventilating, Kyle told himself. *Slow it down.*

With his leg on fire and shivers wracking his body, Kyle was forced to erase the threat above from his mind. At least momentarily. He worked to bring his breathing under control. Each in and out eventually took longer to perform. It was only when the heaving of his chest was almost normal that he turned his focus to his leg. Kyle imagined the damage done. He dreaded taking a look. The stabbing sensation ran from his foot all the way up his thigh.

When he finally worked up the courage to investigate, his leg looked every bit as bad as it felt. One entire side of his pants leg was shredded. Blood seeped through most of the tears. Ribbons of fabric fluttered in the breeze. Through the numbing cold, he felt something trickling down his leg. Blood or stream water, he didn't know. More than likely it was a mix of both.

A rock the size of a golf ball tumbled down the rocky cliff face, landing a few feet from Kyle. He shrunk further against the rock wall. He didn't make a sound. Thankfully, the moonlight failed to reach into the cliff's shadow. For the moment, Kyle felt relatively safe. Safe at least from the eyes of the creature above. *Yellow eyes.* Safe as one could feel while being hunted. Pebbles and snow continued to rain down. Kyle envisioned the hidebehind pacing back and forth along the edge.

Because that's what Kyle had ultimately decided was stalking him: a hidebehind.

You were right, Gabriela. Though it did her little good.

This creature was like none he had ever seen or heard of until now. Large enough to abduct a full-grown human, yet possessing the ability to hide behind narrow trees? The strength to kill, yet move without detection? Kyle couldn't explain it. He only knew what he was up against. He had seen what it could do.

A sour feeling washed over Kyle's stomach. For the first time, defeat seemed not only possible, but inevitable. *Where there had been three, there was now only one.* He wished he had never pulled over. It was his fault. Angelique would still be alive, as would his future sister-in-law. But it was too late for wishes. Angelique wasn't alive and he had doubts about Gabriela.

With the bitter cold numbing every part of Kyle's body except his heartbreak, part of him wanted to lie back and wait. Wait for whatever had happened to Angelique and Gabriela to happen to him. At least then he would have an answer. He would know once and for all what was stalking him.

He almost welcomed that face to face.

With tears once again welling up, an image from the other side of the stream made its way to Kyle's watery eyes. He sat up straight. He used his sleeve to clear his vision. His eyes weren't playing tricks. It wasn't a mirage. The length of ground running alongside the stream appeared shinier than the rest. Reflecting the moonlight, its surface looked slick. It cut a clearing through the trees as far as Kyle could see in either direction.

And this newfound knowledge charged Kyle's battery.

It wasn't the one he had been searching for, but he had found a road alright. Instead of freshly plowed asphalt, this road was made of snow, packed by so many heavy trucks that its surface was smooth and reflective like ice. A service road of some sort. Used by loggers, more than likely. It was a welcome sight, but presented Kyle with a decision to make. Stay hidden or make a break for it?

Even as the question formed, he knew staying wasn't an option. He had to risk it. This was the best opportunity he had been granted so far. And if this road didn't lead to the main road, then so be it. He would give up and simply lay down and wait. Frozen, tired and emotionally distraught, he was at that point. After all, with Angelique gone, all he had left in the world was his dead parent's money and more hangers-on passing themselves off as friends than any one man really needed.

And neither were getting him out of this jam.

Kyle prepared to move. The shower of snow and rock from above had ended minutes ago. Using the cliff face for support, he pulled himself to his feet. It was a struggle and his wince was genuine. The cold air against his exposed skin felt like his ruined leg was being pricked with a million tiny needles. Blood continued to seep from the scrapes.

Kyle leaned out and glanced up at the precipice. The moonlight shed light on the rock ledge. He didn't see anything moving along it.

He turned to the frozen creek bed. He needed a place to cross, so he sought out any small mass of rocks that might act as a bridge. They were few and far between. Random sheets of snow-covered ice populated much of the surface, hiding the flowing stream and any number of submerged obstacles that might reach up and snap an ankle.

Ultimately, the place directly in front of Kyle looked as good a place to cross as any. If for no other reason than he had already tested the depth. Not quite to his knee. The ice had proven fairly thin, so breaking through and finding more solid footing on the streambed wouldn't be an issue. If there were to be an issue, hypothermia and frost bite would be their names.

Kyle blew hot air into his hands.

He rubbed them together.

He placed them against his frozen cheeks and took a deep breath.

His journey began with one step.

When Kyle's boot breached the surface, the percussive crackling of ice shattered the night. The sound echoed off the wall behind him. Kyle shot a frightened glance to the ledge. He expected the hidebehind to appear at the top of the cliff. When it didn't, Kyle wasn't disappointed.

Each cautious step felt colder than the previous as icy water flowed between his feet. The stream rushed more rapidly than Kyle had anticipated. It required deliberate footing. Before he had made it halfway across, the stream sloshed inside his boots and his feet had grown numb.

It took several heart-pounding minutes for Kyle to reach the opposite bank. The step up onto land was a steep one, but doable thanks to a conveniently placed tree root. Kyle exited the stream, frozen but otherwise unharmed. He didn't take time to look back. He threaded his way through the narrow strip of trees separating the road from the stream. Only once he had scaled a small incline and stood with both boots on the icy road did he check the status of matters behind him.

Kyle sucked in a sharp intake of air. His heart leapt into his throat, frightened by what he saw, but not surprised.

Through the trees, a shadow stood at the top of the cliff, watching.

And Kyle moved with a renewed urgency.

The road was makeshift, haphazard and deeply rutted. A small child could have used some of the tire tracks for hide and seek. But, it was a road, nonetheless. Which meant it led *from* somewhere *to* somewhere. Kyle's best guess, a lumbering operation was located on the mountain. He could only hope it was still in operation.

Kyle stuck to the center of the road where the footing was best, constantly checking the landscape behind him. It had only taken a couple of minutes for the hidebehind to join him on his side of the river. It kept pace, hiding behind one tree after another. It never showed more than its shadow. The openness of the road made Kyle feel both secure and vulnerable. He was easy to spot as he limped along. But then so would his stalker be if it made a move.

Thankfully, Kyle's feet were starting to thaw. Feeling was returning, though that feeling was similar to walking on a searing bed of hot coals. He kept his pace as quick as the rutted road and his feet would allow. When he felt more confident in his steps, his walk increased to a light jog. The pain intensified, but he ignored it. There was no other choice. The hidebehind wasn't losing ground. If anything, it was gaining.

Close enough that Kyle could now hear its movements.

The acrid smell of diesel reached Kyle about the same time he heard the low rumble of heavy machinery. It wasn't a pleasant smell, but welcomed nonetheless. His heart rate and pace both accelerated. Where there was machinery, there were usually people there to operate it. And where there were people, Kyle hoped like hell there would be a phone or two-way radio. He dared not get his hopes up. But it was certainly possible and made all the sense in the world.

Rounding a slight bend brought him within eyesight of the operation.

The pyramid of downed logs climbed a good forty feet into the night sky. There had to be a hundred, at least, with ends that were fresh cut. The smell of pine hung in the air like a tree-shaped air freshener, though it failed to overpower the stench of diesel. Large claw marks marred the bark along the trunks of the trees. A fresh layer of snow blanketed the exposed edges.

The clamoring engine was coming from the other side of the woodpile.

As Kyle raced toward the timber, the engine started to sputter. The sound became more intermittent until one final, exhaustive cough announced the end of the machine's tenure. Kyle's spirits raised at the possibility of someone at the helm. Though, it sounded more like the piece of logging equipment had simply run out of gas.

Silence took over. As did Kyle's sense of vulnerability. Looking back only served to heighten that sense. The hide-behind and its shadow were gone. Kyle wasn't relieved in the slightest. He knew better than to think the creature had simply gotten bored and gone home.

Kyle had never been that lucky.

Fresh, undisturbed snow crunched under his boots as Kyle left the smooth surface of the road and made his way around the stack of downed timber. The monolithic beast that had been making all the racket stood before him. Its body, a large black and yellow carriage with one large window eye that wrapped around its entirety. A long claw arm extended off the front. Kyle had seen similar heavy loaders on many of his father's building sites.

The ground beside the loader was, unfortunately, becoming just as familiar.

A man lay sprawled in the middle of a smattering of crimson snow. His arms draped protectively across his abdomen, his legs crossed in a figure four. A yellow hard hat lay half buried in the snow a few feet away. His safety vest remained its original yellow only around the shoulders. From that point down, the man's entire torso was awash in blood. It wasn't until he approached the man that Kyle discovered the reason why: his insides were mostly on the outside, spilling from a gaping hole in his belly.

The crane operator's internal organs jiggled as a coughing fit overtook him.

His eyes were open. Shock kept them that way.

Kyle knelt beside the man. "Where is everybody?"

The man's eyes looked past Kyle as he shook his head. It was subtle and weak, but an acknowledgement nonetheless.

Kyle grabbed the man's hand. "Are you here alone?"

The man nodded, blinking his eyes. When he spoke, his words were accompanied by a gurgling that came from deep in his throat. "Everyone gone. Last truck to town. Nobody else here at ni—"

Another coughing fit stole the ending to the man's sentence. Blood colored spittle flecked his lips, teeth and Van Dyke beard. When the fit ended, it left the man visibly weaker than before. The coughing had zapped what little strength he'd had left. It was a struggle for him to even open his eyes. There was no telling how long the man had hung on like this.

He did not have much longer.

"Dude, hang in there." Kyle squeezed the man's hand. If he was going to get any more information from him, it would need to be soon. "When's the next truck due?"

The man's eyes drifted closed. He mouthed something that Kyle had to interpret.

"Seven o'clock?" Kyle asked.

But the man never confirmed. And he wouldn't speak again. His eyes were closed, his bloody mouth hung slightly slack-jawed. The rising and falling of his chest, faint to begin with, ceased entirely. As far as Kyle could tell, the man was dead.

Kyle sat back, shoulders sagging. If the next truck

wasn't coming until seven in the morning, then somehow, he had to stay alive for several more hours.

It sounded like an impossible task.

Kyle was looking around for a nearby building or structure, someplace that headquartered the operation, when a crashing sound filtered down from overhead. He looked up in time to see a pine log tumbling off the top of the pile. It was heading right for him. His eyes grew in proportion to the log's approach. Kyle scrambled on hands and knees, putting distance between him and the prospective landing area. Snow showered down with each impact as the log bounced off others on its way down.

The log landed with a thunderous roar. It shook the ground, missing Kyle by no more than a couple feet. The dead man wasn't so lucky. A sound similar to a water balloon bursting turned Kyle's stomach. A geyser of blood shot into the air. The shattering of bone joined the sound of splatter.

Stunned, Kyle's eyes turned skyward. Atop the mountain of pine stood a creature only seen in nightmares. It looked like a bear, but was much taller and too skinny. Standing on two legs, it would have resembled a man had its dirty, ashen fur not created an even darker void against the night sky. The eyes. They glowed a toxic yellow. The same yellow Kyle had seen hovering in the tree above Angelique.

The hidebehind hopped off of the top of the pile and onto a jutting log a few feet below.

Kyle screamed.

He didn't have time for much else.

From his backside, Kyle searched for something—a wieldable limb, a rock—anything to fend off the creature. But only small sticks populated the area. Kyle looked to the man who now lay mostly hidden underneath the large piece of timber. Only his lower legs were exposed. But that was enough. Kyle saw something near the man's ankle that gave him hope. It glinted in the moonlight.

A gun.

Strapped to a pale ankle inside a small black holster.

Kyle scrambled back to the dead man, who apparently hadn't had time to defend himself.

His loss. Kyle's gain.

The hidebehind landed on its feet just behind Kyle. He could hear the creature's heavy breathing. He could feel the heat from its breath against his neck.

Kyle dove onto the man's lifeless legs.

The Velcro tore away noisily as Kyle wrenched the gun free from its holster. He rolled onto his back and swung the gun around. The creature ducked away. Kyle's shot missed wide.

Searing pain ripped through Kyle's stomach as the creature slashed at it with a talon-like claw. Kyle wailed. The warmth of blood pooling inside his ski jacket proved an odd sensation. After all, he was so cold.

Kyle squeezed the trigger a second time. Again, the bullet missed its mark.

Raising its head high, the creature opened its jaws wider than should have been possible. Something in them had come unhinged. A shriek erupted from its throat, but not a shriek of pain. A shriek of rage. Its yellow eyes flashed wildly before rolling up into its head. Blood glistened on the matted fur around its cavernous mouth. Stringy flesh from its last meal remained caught in its razor-like teeth.

The open jaws catapulted downward and clamped shut onto Kyle's stomach. When the creature reared its head back, chunks of Kyle's jacket, skin and muscle tore away with it.

Kyle screamed, now in agony.

He pulled the trigger. This time he was too overcome. The gun wasn't even aimed at the creature. Kyle's arm fell limp to his side, taking the gun with it. He could do nothing to stop the creature from feasting on his insides. And what a surreal sight it was, seeing its head buried in his abdomen, ingesting what they both needed to live.

Kyle's last moments were filled with thoughts of Angelique and Gabriela. And of how much the creature's breath smelled of coppery blood and too much cheap perfume.

———

It seems the sasquatch has a smaller, lesser-known cousin that most people have never heard of. As this story states, a hidebehind is a creature in American folklore believed to roam the woods and forests in mountainous regions of the United States. It stands as tall as a man, can make itself thin enough to hide behind the slimmest of trees, and feasts on the intestines of those who wander the woods. They apparently have a special fondness for the intestines found inside loggers. So how is it that this creature is not more well-known? And what other beings share our world without our knowledge?

Skull Session

"How are your knees?" the woman asks, entering the workshop.

The man's eyes don't stray from the femur in his hand. He rubs it with a heavily-soaked rag. A bottle of hydrogen peroxide sits on the workbench in front of him. "My knees?"

"Are they in praying shape?" the woman asks. "I mean, if it comes to that."

The man's laugh is deep and fills the room like toxic gas. He turns to the woman, tilts his head down and eyes her over his black rim glasses. "Can't say I've ever been the prayin' type. You should know that." He returns to polishing the leg bone. "Why do you ask?"

"Cuz if this guy doesn't pan out," the woman picks up the bottle of hydrogen peroxide and replaces the lid, "we're fucked. Barnes gave us til the end of the month before he took his business elsewhere. Not only was Tuesday the end of the month, but we've already spent his money."

The man contemplates the bone in his hand. "And our reputation goes to shit."

"Forget our reputation," the woman says. "You've heard the rumors about Barnes. About the girls? The man is dangerous."

The man sucks in his lower lip, holds it and releases. "This guy's gonna pan out. Sounds like he's got just what Barnes is looking for. Right down to the impact damage." The man lays the femur onto a thin, rectangular pillow covered in black felt. "Just as long as it's a male specimen, which he claims it is, everything should be fine."

The woman looks at the clock on the wall across the room. "And if it's not?"

"Well, then, I guess we'll have to improvise."

The woman casts her eyes downward and nods. She sets the bottle on a shelf above the workbench, well aware of what the man means by improvising. She's not excited by the prospect, but also sees no other options. "He should be here in about an hour."

The man rises from his stool and walks over to a wash basin in the corner. He turns on the faucet. "Then I guess we better get things ready, just in case."

———

Jørn stands on the stoop of 169 Saul Avenue and looks up at the redbrick brownstone with an antique wrought iron portico. The wooden door is tall and looks heavy with its ornate stained-glass inserts running down the sides. Mounted just above the peephole is a simple black metal sign with gold trim and deep red lettering:

Infernales.

Wedged in the middle of a long line of brick facades, most

passersby wouldn't even know a store was nestled among the row of townhouses. Certainly, the small and nondescript sign would only catch so many eyes. Jørn runs his hand down the length of his manicured beard and wonders what the neighbors would think of the wares housed inside. Judging by the way the high-end imports outnumber the domestics parked along the tree-lined street, he can't imagine they would be fans. The quaint neighborhood is typical of every one he has seen in American cinema. It is not Jørn's world. In fact, it couldn't be more opposite from his childhood home in Norway. Large flowerpots line the sidewalk, overflowing with color. Tightly sculpted trees dot the curbside every twenty feet. Even the neighborhood of Flatbush where he shares an apartment with his bass player is nothing like this place.

A layer of sweat coats Jørn's pale, freshly shaved head. The afternoon is bright and painful and he is reminded why he rarely ventures out during the day. Trips like this seldom become necessary. Tucked in the crook of his arm he carries an object wrapped in a black cloth. He was wrong to ever buy it and is eager to be rid of it.

The tinkling of a bell announces his entrance. Jørn gently closes the door behind him. Black and red curtains hang over the two windows that straddle the door, blocking out the sun. Jørn slides his sunglasses up to the top of his head and feels his eyes relax. His green eyes that everyone seems to think are so cool. The music floating through the store is soft and atmospheric. It is not a melody he is familiar with, though he appreciates its creepy-ness. The background chants are subtle and a nice touch.

A counter sits unattended at the far end of the narrow and congested living room turned novelty shop. The rest of the space is taken up by a world too fantastical to have been created from just one imagination.

While Jørn waits to be helped, he is torn between

which oddities to start with first. The turn of the century leather satchels with their crude saws and hooked knives that look more like torture devices than medical kits to his left, or the various collection of jars full of piss-colored fluid and masses of white tissue to his right. He has seen his share of medieval medical kits, so Jørn turns to his right.

Several jars sit side by side on a shelf. One, the size of a large pickle jar, appears to contain the remains of a miniature two-headed piglet. Its skin is a milky white. Pieces of it hang free from the rest of the body like soggy bread. One of its misshapen faces presses against the glass. Jørn leans in closer and taps at it. He has heard about such treasures, but has never seen them up close.

"Drood's gotta see this place."

He chooses not to even consider the price tag hanging around the jar's wide neck.

Beside the shelf of pickled specimens sits something even more intriguing. Four small masses of wrinkled skin and hair stand out from the other knick-knacks displayed atop a glass case full of creepy porcelain dolls. The objects resemble balls of some sort, only these are not a child's plaything. Jørn carefully picks up the smallest of the shrunken heads and turns it over in his hand. The head is lighter than he suspected, its stiff hair a dark brown. The lips and eyelids are stitched with thread, keeping them both closed. Small orange and white beads hang from the ears. Attached to the backs are loops of twine, apparently for hanging, though Jørn has no idea why.

"That would be one ugly ass Christmas tree," Jørn says to the suit of armor standing nearby.

A shuffling sound from a back room draws Jørn's attention from the shrunken head. He remembers why he is here in the first place.

At the back of the store, a curtain of stringed beads parts and a petite woman with long pink hair and blunt bangs emerges through a doorway. Her black shawl is stitched with silver Celtic knots and trails behind her as she steps over to the counter. It looks homemade, as does the wide black choker around her throat. Jørn doesn't recognize the symbol on the silver pendant hanging from the center, but it looks official enough. Black eyeliner shadows her eyes against her soft white face.

She is very much the type of woman Jørn finds himself drawn to, and he wonders if she has ever seen his band, Necromancer.

"May I help you?"

Jørn returns the shrunken head to the display case and approaches the counter. He offers a smile and sets the black bundle on the glass top. It elicits a dull thud. "I called earlier?"

The woman twists the pendant hanging from her choker. She bites her ruby red bottom lip. "Ah, yes," she says. "The Viking skull."

Jørn nods, sliding the bundle across the counter.

The woman's hand disappears below the counter before reappearing a second later. Her lips curl into a weak smile as she pulls the bundle closer. Carefully, she unwraps the cloth and spreads it out on the counter. When she's done, a skull sits in the middle of the black fabric. It is white, human, and verifiably real. The temple is crushed on one side. The gaping hole is the size of a golf ball. All but two of the teeth remain intact on both the top and bottom jaws.

A shiver snakes its way down Jørn's spine at the sight of it.

"Ah," she says again, leaning in. "Where did you say you got this?"

"Online." Jørn shoves his hands into the front pockets of his black jeans. "I bought it from a website that specializes in bones."

The woman picks up the skull with delicate hands. Her fingernails are long and black and make clacking sounds as they come in contact with the bony surface. "And why, may I ask are you wanting to part with such a beautiful specimen?"

Jørn shrugs, recalling the argument he'd made for buying the piece in the first place. "I thought it would be cool to have, ya know? Keep it on my coffee table, give it a name. Maybe use it onstage when I sing. But, once I got it, I don't know, it just…it kinda creeps me out. More than I thought it would. I mean, I'm into dark and mysterious shit, but this thing's just a little too real."

"I see." The woman turns the skull carefully in her hands, inspecting all its nooks and crannies. She peers into the cavernous eye sockets like she's searching for the soul that once inhabited the skull. She pulls it closer for a better look at the smashed temple. The woman runs a slender finger along the jagged edges of the cavity. She again bites her bottom lip as she studies.

Jørn can't help but let his attention wander. There is almost too much to see. On the wall behind the counter, faded sideshow banners hang on display. They appear vintage and portray advertisements of the usual turn of the century carnival fare: a man in a loincloth lies atop a bed of nails while another man in a suit stands on his chest; the Tattooed Girl of Shang-Ri-La, whose entire body is decorated in color, lays sprawled on a white Victorian sofa, her privates strategically covered. A third banner, advertising live demonstrations by Sadie the Sword Swallower, interests Jørn, but the $225 price tag does not.

"The website said the Viking was killed by a sword to the head," Jørn offers.

The woman spends another few seconds closely examining the fracture before gently setting the skull back onto the cloth.

"Well," she says, looking at Jørn with pity in her eyes, "the website lied."

Jørn's brow furrows. "What do you mean?"

"Well, there are three tell-tale signs," she says. "For starters, this fracture wasn't caused by a sword. It's much too large of a cavity. This damage was caused by something larger and more blunt. Something with a little heft. I'd suspect a club of some sort. Maybe even an axe or a hammer."

Jørn's eyes narrow.

"Trust me," the woman says, reading his mind, "I spent two years studying Forensic Pathology. I've seen my share of blunt force traumas."

Jørn is not entirely swayed. He clutches his beard in a loose fist just below the chin and strokes the length of it down to its pointed end near the center of his chest. "It's probably just a guess on their part anyway. No one can know for sure how the Viking actually died. It was a long time ago."

"And that's lie number two." The woman clicks her fingernail a couple times on the crown of the skull. "It's too clean. Too white. There's no aging on this skull. If it were indeed a thousand years old, it would have a nice beige or sandy patina. Especially if it's been stored in no better vessel than this. Which, I'm assuming, it has not been."

The creases on Jørn's brow grow deeper. Subconsciously, he takes a step away from the counter. He sees dollar signs being flushed down a toilet the more the conversation drones on. "Are you sure?"

"Besides my forensic studies, I've seen just about every bone in the human body come through that door. And more than any other, I've seen my share of skulls." The woman folds her arms across her chest. "Yes, I'm sure."

The clomping of heavy footsteps comes from above. The woman seems not to notice, but the heaviness of the steps pique Jørn's curiosity. Each step sounds like it's being made by a combat boot filled with lead.

"Did you know we have a congresswoman who's trying to make it illegal to possess human bones in the state of New York?"

Jørn shakes his head.

"Yep," the woman continues. "With the exception of using them for medical purposes."

Jørn is not sure what to say. He could care less about some congresswoman and what she is trying to do. He has obviously been duped. A sense of embarrassment comes over him. If all that the woman is telling him is true, then it is no wonder that all sales are final according to the website.

He is afraid to find out, but Jørn asks the question anyway.

"What's the third sign?"

"Huh?" The woman's focus is clearly somewhere else.

"You said there were three tell-tale signs that the website lied to me."

The woman nods, her train of thought coming back to the skull. "I'm sorry, but this ain't even the skull of a grown man. It's much too small and the bone itself is too thin. And you see this faint line right here? Runs along the temporal line. If this skull belonged to a man, the line would be much more pronounced. More of a ridge." The woman's shoulders deflate. She lets out a sigh. "Unfortu-nately, this skull belonged to a young woman. Maybe even a teenage girl. And not at all what we're looking for."

Jørn's stomach sours. Feelings of both anger and fear set in. How stupid was he, wasting his money on such a crock of shit? Even as he sat at the library's computer, he feared he would one day regret the purchase.

But Jørn has more to worry about than buyer's remorse. What is the woman telling him? That this skull is most likely from a young woman who was recently killed with an axe or hammer? What are the implications? And what the hell does that mean for him?

The heavy footfalls return, this time louder. Closer. The curtain of stringed beads parts. The largest man Jørn has ever seen pushes his way through. Standing well over the height of a normal human being, the man has to duck his oversized head so as not to bang it on the doorway. But he isn't just tall. The man's broad shoulders also push the limits of the doorway's opening. He has to turn a little in order to squeeze through. A sharp contrast to the rather petite woman, this man gives new meaning to the phrase "mountain of a man."

The man steps behind the counter and nods his boulder of a head in Jørn's direction. "Afternoon." The man's voice is so deep, it reverberates in Jørn's chest. The man reminds him of a James Bond nemesis.

And people say Jørn looks intimidating.

"Hey," Jørn says, unable to tear his eyes from the man. The man sports a raven-black tailcoat with a deep red and black button up vest underneath. His long black hair is pulled into a ponytail, and behind black-rimmed glasses, his eyes have the same shadowy look as the woman's. Jørn doesn't catch a glimpse of the man's boots, but he envi-sions them to be just as clunky and metallic as the many rings and chains the man wears. Steel buckles are a safe bet.

"Is this it?" The man's eyes are alive with excitement.

The woman turns and hands the skull to the man as carefully as if it were made of the world's most expensive crystal. The man brings the skull up to his face for a closer look. Turning it over in his massive hands, it is the hole in the temple that draws the intake of breath.

"Ever read any Edward Lee?" When Jørn shakes his head, the man says, "no matter." He brings the skull close to his nose and sniffs the air. His eyes drift closed. "Exquisite."

A shiver runs down Jørn's neck. He can't imagine what scent the man is pulling off of the bone. He doesn't recall it having a particular smell. But then perhaps his olfactory sense isn't as acute to such things. Certainly not a bad thing. The man's continued fascination with the jagged hole in the skull stirs Jørn's stomach.

The man looks to the woman, licks his lips and asks, "Male?"

The woman hesitates, then shakes her head. She casts her eyes downward.

"So." Jørn is disappointed by the news, but eager to be rid of the purchase. "It is still a skull, right? It's gotta be worth something to you."

"It is," the woman says, lifting her head. "But, we really were counting on it being the skull of a male. Honestly, I had my doubts about it actually being Viking, but hoped at least…" The woman lets the rest of the sentence trail off.

The man sets the skull onto the counter. The excitement is gone from his eyes. He turns to the woman. "You wanna check the faucet for me? Can't remember if I turned it off."

The woman looks at the man, then to Jørn, then back

to the man. Her eyes are suddenly filled with a sadness that Jørn can't place. "Sure."

Both men watch as the woman disappears through the beaded curtain.

In contrast to the mood, the music being pumped through the store turns upbeat. It catches Jørn's attention. "A Means to an End" by Joy Division. He knows the song well.

"So," Jørn says to the man, breaking the silence between them, "if you're not interested, do you know someone who might be?"

"Maybe." The man offers nothing more to the conversation. He looks toward the beaded curtain. A moment later, he turns back to Jørn. "Wanna see something cool?"

Jørn looks around the shop for a clock. "I don't know, I probably need—"

"Seriously," the man interrupts. "If you're into crazy shit, you'll love this."

"Really?"

The man nods. The beginning of a smile emerges. "It doesn't get much crazier, I assure you."

Jørn shrugs. It's clear he is not getting out of the store until he appeases the man. Not if he wants some cash in his pocket. "Alright."

The man steps over to the beaded curtain and pulls it back. "Come on back."

Jørn steps behind the counter and through the curtain. A short hallway awaits. The sound of their boots on the linoleum echoes off the drab white walls, the man's louder than Jørn's. He can hear the man's heavy breathing behind him.

"First doorway on your right."

When he approaches the open doorway, Jørn's pace slows. *Is this crazy?* He glances back at the man who smiles and nods encouragement. When he turns the corner and steps through the doorway, Jørn is taken aback by what he sees.

Sheets of clear plastic adorn the walls. They drape over what appears to be a workbench. Strips of shelf-like wood are stacked about, holding the plastic in place. Plastic covers the floor. It crinkles under his boots when Jørn steps into the room.

Alarms go off in Jørn's head.

He shouldn't be here.

This isn't right.

As he takes a step backward, Jørn backs into the man. Before he can turn around, he is shoved from behind. He stumbles deeper into the brightly-lit room, but maintains his footing.

Jørn spins. "What the—"

A shout comes from his left. As Jørn turns in that direction, the woman charges at him. She clutches one of the shelves in her hands, raised above her head. Jørn's eyes widen. Before he can react further, she swings the board downward.

The wood emits a powerful cracking sound as it connects with the back of Jørn's skull. A bright light blinds him, but only for a second. Something behind his right eye tears. More sharp pain from that area. When the blinding light recedes, Jørn is left disoriented. He stumbles. Something is wrong with his vision.

"Holy shit, Rae Ann!" It is the man's voice. It booms in the tiny room. "That was some shot!" Laughter. "And he's still standing!"

Jørn's attention shifts toward the voice, his feet shuffling.

A gasp from the woman.

A raucous hoot from the man.

"Mother of God," the man chortles. "Would ya look at that!"

Jørn staggers a couple of steps, his vision still not right. He can see well enough out of his right eye, but it's his left that is off. The floor is all it sees no matter where he tries to focus it. The effect is dizzying and Jørn feels bile rise up in his throat.

Another whoosh cuts through the air.

Another shot to the back of Jørn's head. This time the wood splinters and sheers. Large shards of wood clatter to the floor as Jørn drops to a knee. His thoughts turn muddy. His vision betrays him. A warm trickle of blood runs from his ear.

The man steps up to Jørn, who swats at him with weak arms. The man deflects the blows without effort. He reaches up toward Jørn's face.

Jørn draws back.

But it's too late.

Thick meaty fingers enclose around the vision in Jørn's left eye.

The man laughs. "It's just fuckin' hangin' there, Rae Ann. Ever seen anything like it?" With a jerk of his hand, a sickening sound like the slurping of a straw. Jørn's optic nerve tears. His eyeball comes free.

Jørn wails. Spritzes of blood warm his cheek. Darkness cloaks the spot where his left eye used to see. Pain rockets up into his brain. From his right eye, Jørn watches as the man raises Jørn's eyeball to his own and marvels.

"Fuckin' beautiful!" The man shakes his head in wonder. "Don't see 'em in green very often."

Throughout it all, the woman has remained silent. Wavering from side to side, Jørn looks to her for help.

She stands frozen, a sheered piece of wood still gripped in her hands. Her expression is one of shellshock. Her mouth hangs open. Her wide eyes dart back and forth from Jørn to the bloody eyeball in the man's hand. The plastic sheet on the floor crinkles as she backs away.

Jørn reaches for her. "Please."

The woman drops the piece of wood. Turning, she rushes from the room.

A wave of dizziness washes over Jørn. He must use both hands on the floor to stabilize himself and remain upright. Wooden shrapnel litters the plastic, poking his palms. He tries to rise to his feet, but he's too unsteady. His stomach lets go of its contents.

The man takes a step back, removing himself from the splash zone. The whimsical smile leaves his face. "Thank God and Home Depot for plastic sheeting." The man sets Jørn's eyeball on the workbench. He casts his gaze down upon Jørn. "Sorry, my brother, but duty calls. Nothing personal. I just need that skull of yours."

The man reaches behind his back. Drawing his arm upward produces a unique and familiar sound. A blade being pulled from its sheath. And a rather long blade by the sound of it.

Jørn's blood runs cold. His mind begins systematically running through options, but his thoughts are cloudy and they come sluggishly.

When the man's hand reappears, it holds a long, pointed sword with a broad blade. He turns it this way and that, wielding the heavy sword effortlessly. The muscles in his thick forearm twist back and forth.

Jørn takes in the antique piece of weaponry, but his eye struggles to focus. His gut lurches. He draws in a deep breath. The back of his skull throbs with its own pulse.

"You like that?" the man asks, showing off the sword like a prize. "It's called a *gladius*. Roman. Old as shit."

When the man moves the sword closer for Jørn to get a

better look, Jørn turns his head away. On the floor, his hands enclose around two very long and shrewdly shorn shards of wood. The edges dig into his palms, adding his hands to the list of body parts in pain. But this pain he can live with.

"I promise," the man starts to draw his arm back, "it'll be quick. But I can't guarantee painless."

Using all of the strength he has, Jørn lunges forward, bringing up both fists. The sharp ends of the makeshift spikes pierce the skin of the man's forearm. One enters from the inside, the other from the outside. Somewhere among tissue, muscle and bone, the pointed ends pass each other before exiting in the opposite direction.

The man's cry of agony is painful to Jørn's ears. But music, no less. The sword clangs to the floor before Jørn. When the man yanks his arm away, Jørn releases the pieces of wood. Four bloody sections of wood plank protrude from the man's forearm. Blood spurts from each wound. He grabs his forearm with his other hand and gawks at the insolence.

Jørn springs from his crouch. He rushes forward, driving his shoulder square into the man's mammoth gut. The man's feet scatter for purchase as Jørn drives him against the wall.

The air in the man's lungs exit in one swift outward blast.

Jørn steps back from the man, his energy spent, his stability wavering. With a hand to the back of his head, he stumbles toward the open doorway, nearly getting his feet caught up in the plastic sheet. He exits into the hall, expecting the woman to be there waiting. She is nowhere to be found.

Jørn makes his way down the short hallway using the walls for support. He leaves a trail of splattered blood in his wake. Hand prints on the walls. Random splatters on the floor. His boots drag along the linoleum, smearing the blood and tracking it through the store.

At the front door, Jørn turns and steals a look behind him. Neither the man nor woman have mounted a pursuit. Only the bellows of the injured man have followed him. When they die, Jørn can hear the woman's frantic inquiries.

The sun hits Jørn like a city bus. He squints away the pain, but relishes being out of the store. He takes the stairs cautiously, holding onto the railing with slippery hands. The sounds of the subway remind him which direction he came. He turns left at the bottom of the stairs and puts as much distance between him and the store as he can, as quickly as his wobbly legs can manage. Moments later, Jørn leaves the neighborhood with less than when he arrived, and he doesn't look back.

———

Three weeks later, the man turns the screwdriver with his good hand. He holds the black and gold sign in place with the palm of his other hand. It a task that would have been simpler if his fingers weren't useless. Now, they only seem to get in the way. Only a couple more turns and the screw tightens against the metal plate, securing it to the iron bars that protect the glass door. The man steps back and admires his new storefront, sign and all.

The volume of traffic on the street behind him— pedestrians, cars, motorcycles, buses, food vendors—drives him into the shop. The closing of the door silences the outside world. He likes the quiet inside his world. The familiar and the bizarre.

As he passes through the store, he nods to a couple of

young locals perusing the various oddities that line the new shelves.

"Hey, Juan," he hears one of them say. "Check out this eyeball in this jar. It's fuckin' green, *Esé*."

The man smiles and continues to the back of the store. He joins the woman behind the counter. "We're gonna do well here," he says. "You'll see."

The woman straightens a stack of freshly-printed business cards. "I still worry."

The man nods. "I know." He rests his good hand on the woman's shoulder. "But the guy brought us the skull of a recently murdered young woman. I don't think he's going to the police. At least he hasn't yet." He removes his hand from her shoulder. "Besides," he spreads his arms wide, "viva Mexico, am I right?"

The two Mexican men enthusiastically return the salutation.

The man smiles, winks at the woman and passes through a beaded curtain into his clean, new workshop.

About the Author

A graduate of Otterbein College, Tim McWhorter is the author of the horror/thrillers *Shadows Remain*, *Bone White*, *Blackened*. He lives just outside of Columbus, OH, with his wife, a dwindling number of children and a few obligatory 'family' pets that have somehow become solely his responsibility. He is currently hard at work on something altogether disturbing and relies on interaction with readers to keep him from going over the edge…

www.timmcwhorter.com

tm5to1@live.com

Also by Tim McWhorter

Bone White

Blackened

The Winding Down Hours

Shadows Remain

Swallowing the Worm and Other Stories

www.ingramcontent.com/pod-product-compliance
Lightning Source LLC
Chambersburg PA
CBHW070000200626
46811CB00021B/2877